She was impossible to forget.

Looking at those big blue eyes that were staring at him with recognition and horror, he felt memories slam into him.

He hadn't seen her since he was sixteen, when she'd been his persistent shadow. The bane of his existence. "Chloe? What are you doing here?"

She blushed. "I—I thought you were in the military. Your family said—"

Apparently her memories of him weren't that happy, either. "I've been back a couple days. They were expecting me."

"I…um…I'm renting a cabin here on the ranch. For a few months."

He gaped. "Months?" he repeated, hoping he'd heard her wrong.

She nodded as she grabbed her suitcase. "Well…I guess I'd better get settled."

Of all people to show up while he was trying to regain a sense of peace and figure out how to start his life over!

As he watched her enter the cabin, he couldn't help f   on a fragile preci   water below. F Chloe's eyes.

A *USA TODAY* bestselling and award-winning author of over thirty-five novels, **Roxanne Rustand** lives in the country with her husband and a menagerie of pets, including three horses, rescue dogs and cats. She has a master's in nutrition and is a clinical dietitian. *RT Book Reviews* nominated her for a Career Achievement Award, two of her books won their annual Reviewers' Choice Award and two others were nominees.

Books by Roxanne Rustand

Love Inspired

Rocky Mountain Ranch

Montana Mistletoe
High Country Homecoming

Aspen Creek Crossroads

Winter Reunion
Second Chance Dad
The Single Dad's Redemption
An Aspen Creek Christmas
Falling for the Rancher

Rocky Mountain Heirs

The Loner's Thanksgiving Wish

Love Inspired Suspense

Big Sky Secrets

Fatal Burn
End Game
Murder at Granite Falls
Duty to Protect

Visit the Author Profile page at Harlequin.com for more titles.

High Country Homecoming

Roxanne Rustand

Recycling programs
for this product may
not exist in your area.

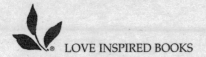

LOVE INSPIRED BOOKS

ISBN-13: 978-1-335-47921-1

High Country Homecoming

Copyright © 2019 by Roxanne Rustand

www.Harlequin.com

Printed in U.S.A.

Charity suffereth long, and is kind; charity envieth not; charity vaunteth not itself, is not puffed up, Doth not behave itself unseemly, seeketh not her own, is not easily provoked, thinketh no evil; Rejoiceth not in iniquity, but rejoiceth in the truth; Beareth all things, believeth all things, hopeth all things, endureth all things. Charity never faileth.

—*1 Corinthians* 13:4–8

With love to Danielle, Ben, Lily, Violet and Finn.
You light up my life!

Chapter One

Home. Sort of, anyway.

Chloe Kenner glanced down the hill toward the sprawling ranch-style home sheltered by pines, then scanned the horse and cattle barns far below. Assured that no one was watching, she did a happy dance of joy.

She'd lived on the Langfords' remote Montana ranch for five years as a little girl, while following her dad from his erratic employment at one ranch to the next. Even though their abrupt departure had been clouded with the usual embarrassment and regret, she still had warm memories of two of the three Langford boys and their sweet grandma, Betty.

The middle brother—Devlin—was another story altogether. But when she'd called to ask about renting a cabin, Betty had said Devlin was career military and rarely visited. And though everyone would be gone when Chloe hoped to arrive, her isolated cabin would be unlocked and ready, and she was to make herself at home.

Perfect. Complete peace and quiet.

After the calamitous end of her secretarial job in

Minneapolis, heavy local news coverage of the debacle had ensured that she was nearly unemployable there. At least until one particularly rabid reporter gave up and decided to leave her in peace, and all of the others forgot about her and moved on. But surely none of them would find her clear out here in Montana.

She'd been skillfully framed by her conniving former boss—who had lied about being single and had declared his undying love, while embezzling from investment clients, then he'd pinned the crime on her when he was caught. How had she been so blind? Such a poor judge of character? Just the thought of ever risking another romance made her shudder.

But the thought of looming bankruptcy was worse. With no interruptions for the next three months, she could finish her writing projects and pray they would help pay off her staggering legal debts.

She shifted the weight of her heavy backpack, bowed her head and resolutely dragged her bulky suitcase up the rocky trail to the first of three cabins that she remembered were strewn amongst the trees.

The unfamiliar higher elevation had her panting as she struggled onward, but the crisp pine scent was so sharp and pure, so reminiscent of the past, she knew she was already grinning from ear to ear when she finally caught sight of a cabin partly hidden by the trees to the right.

Pebbles skittered down the steep path far ahead of her. A twig snapped.

Her heart lurched. She drew in a sharp breath, her eyes riveted on the trail that wound through some boulders and disappeared into the trees.

Bears.

Mountain lions.

Even wolves were possible here, in the foothills of the Rockies. She eyed the distance to the cabin. *Too far.* Running might make her look like scared, easy prey. Like a big, tasty rabbit.

She eased her backpack onto one shoulder and pulled the suitcase alongside her hip to widen her profile, raised her arms to look more intimidating, and then as a forewarning, began belting out the only song she could think of.

Another twig snapped.

A tall form sauntered into view, backlit by early evening sun. She couldn't make out his features, yet she instantly knew who he was. *Trouble.* The song died on her lips as she blinked and swallowed hard.

If only it had been a bear.

"'Jingle bells'?" Devlin drawled.

Bright flags of color turned the young woman's face as pink as the roses his late mother had planted along the front of the main ranch house, turning her into a riot of color with that fluorescent-yellow T-shirt and the cloud of curly dark auburn hair that had partly escaped her ponytail. Several silver bracelets gleamed on her right wrist.

His first thought was that he'd like to get to know her a whole lot better.

His second was that a woman like this one wouldn't want to be seen with someone like him. Six months ago, maybe. But not anymore.

He searched her face, his gut telling him that he knew her. From high school? College? Maybe an old neighbor? After so many years in the military, he'd lost touch with everyone around here.

Yet a lovely woman like this one would be impossible to forget, with that delicate ivory complexion, playful scattering of small freckles across her nose, and big blue eyes the size of pansies that were now looking up at him with recognition and utter horror.

A cascade of memories tinged with guilt slammed through his thoughts.

He hadn't seen her since he was sixteen and she'd been his spindly, persistent shadow. An eleven-year-old chatterbox who had been the bane of his existence. "Chloe?"

"I—I thought you were in the Marines," she stammered, her blush deepening. "Betty said…"

Apparently her memories of him weren't that happy, either. "I've been back just a of couple days. They weren't expecting me."

She swallowed hard, her gaze sliding past him. "I… um… I'm renting a cabin here. For a few months."

He stared at her, at a loss for words.

While the family was piling into his brother Jess's SUV to leave for California yesterday morning, Betty had mentioned that someone was coming to stay in the cabin nearest the house.

He could now guess why she'd conveniently neglected to say who it was, or for how long. Betty had always seemed to know Devlin better than he knew himself, and surely she'd seen how Chloe had pestered him all those years ago.

But he still couldn't imagine why the renter had to be this Pollyanna, who could cheerfully talk nonstop for hours without taking a breath. What on earth would she do with herself on this lonely, isolated ranch? Bother him, no doubt.

Pine Bend, Montana, population 1,200, was a good fifteen miles away, and the town beyond was another twenty miles, with even fewer residents.

"Months?" he repeated, hoping he'd heard her wrong—which was always a possibility, given his battle-damaged hearing.

She nodded as she shifted the weight of her backpack and grabbed the handle of her suitcase. "Well, then… I guess I'd better get settled."

His vision of blessed, healing solitude evaporated. Sure, there were others living here at the ranch, but none of them were intrusive, and even his brother's six-year-old twins seemed to sense that he needed to be left alone.

The Chloe he remembered had no such sense of personal boundaries.

He sighed, giving in to the inevitable. Dad had bought up several neighboring ranches at foreclosure auctions before he passed away. Maybe Devlin could use one of those houses if any were vacant.

Still, the strict code of manners instilled in him since childhood nudged at him. "Do you need help with that luggage?"

She shook her head and veered off the trail, onto the path toward the cabin, clearly laboring against the weight of that ridiculously large suitcase and the steep incline.

She was still stubborn, too.

He silently strode over to her and took the handle, carried the bag up to the cabin and opened the door wide.

He surveyed the interior, which was in far better

condition than the other two cabins up the hill that had been empty for years. Betty had clearly done her best to make this one welcoming.

The windows were open to let in the crisp mountain air, a Mason jar on the table held a bouquet of wildflowers and through the open bedroom door, he could see a stack of fresh towels waiting on a bright patchwork quilt. The hardwood floors gleamed.

Chloe came inside behind him and dropped her backpack by the door with a soft gasp of wonder. "It's almost the same as when I was a girl."

She stood close enough that he heard almost every word clearly before she walked into the center of the main room and turned slowly, taking in the stone fireplace, the pine paneling, the sofa draped with a quilt and the dark pine rocking chair in the corner. Beyond an L-shaped counter with a breakfast bar and three bar stools, the rustic pine cabinets and updated kitchen appliances gleamed.

"This was always the foreman's cabin, but I hear the last one left last November. Looks like Jess has done quite a bit of work in here." He backed toward the open door and spun on his heel to leave.

At the touch of Chloe's hand on his sleeve, he froze.

"Thank you," she said. "This will be perfect."

He nodded and made his escape without turning his right side toward her, avoiding the inevitable for a little while longer.

Initially, he'd been self-conscious, and had become adept at concealing his scars with collared, long-sleeved shirts and by the way he angled his face away during a conversation.

Now it was just a reflex.

For the most part, he'd learned to mask his more invisible and aggravating losses. The significant loss of his hearing, even with hearing aids. Loss of perfect vision in his right eye.

But even though he no longer cared what people thought of his appearance, he did dread the automatic gush of sympathy and empty platitudes from strangers who could surely care less.

But it was all relative.

Seeing Chloe again brought back his dark, helpless sense of being damaged, though his war injuries didn't hold a candle to the crushing burden of what had happened on this ranch when he was just a kid.

Why did she have to show up while he was trying to start his life over?

Until last spring he'd been a Marine, an invincible warrior in control of his life. Now he was a disfigured man with disabilities, with nightmares that could hit without warning.

He'd spent the past six months recovering from multiple surgeries, knowing the military would never take him back for active duty. But last month, that sense of hopelessness had changed, thanks to an old buddy from the Marines who recommended him for a job. A *perfect* job.

And so he'd applied for a field position with a nationally acclaimed, high-tech security company. The recruiter had been doubtful, wondering if Devlin was still capable, but had given him until the first of July to prove he could handle the job.

And Devlin *would* do it. No question.

He would focus on regaining his strength, his dexterity. His accuracy with a weapon. And by July 1 he would be packing his bags for New York so his could reclaim his life, and a future. Having a firm goal had given him a new sense of hope.

But now, with Chloe's arrival, instead of peace, he felt as if he were wavering on a fragile precipice with unknown, dangerous water below.

Was it the memory of her endlessly cheerful smile? The way she'd always tried to convince him that everything in his world was rosy, when as a young boy he was dealing with grief and guilt that never faded and a father who...

Even without hearing her footsteps, he sensed her coming up behind him. Stifling a sigh, he stopped in his tracks and spun around to face her.

"Look, I know we weren't exactly friends when my dad was the foreman here. In fact," she added with a rueful smile, "I suspect I was an awful pest."

That much was true.

She'd shadowed his every move and asked a million questions every day, so in return he'd learned to retaliate by being a relentless tease—taunting her about her carrot-red hair, her freckles, her skinny legs—anything to just make her go away.

Never in a million years would he have told her that her hair was the prettiest color he'd ever seen, or that he'd always thought her freckles were cute. Looking back on his cruel younger self, he felt a flash of remorse.

"We were just kids. And you were almost like a sis—" he stumbled over the word.

"Sister," she said softly, her eyes all too knowing. "I never knew the right things to say. But I saw the pain you and your brothers went through after your little sister died. And how cruel your dad was to you boys afterward. I just wanted to make things better somehow. Instead I probably drove you all crazy."

His sense of guilt sharpened.

Life hadn't been easy for her either, with an alcoholic father and a mother who'd ditched them both. Yet there she'd been, a little girl earnestly trying to help everyone else at the ranch after Heather's death. Grandma Betty had called her a pint-size Pollyanna, but in return, he hadn't been kind at all.

"Um… I can see my arrival is a surprise," she added with a fleeting, wistful smile. "But don't worry. I'll be working in my cabin, making my own meals, and I won't be a bother. You'll hardly ever see me. Promise."

The impact of her words hit him like a fist to the gut.

He'd put in his latest set of hearing aids from the VA this morning to give them one last try—though they sure didn't help much and were aggravating to boot. Now he almost wished he hadn't, because her meaning was all too clear. She figured making herself invisible was the best way to make him happy, and the sad part was that she was right.

Feeling like a jerk, he started to dredge up an apology, but she walked away without turning back.

After finishing up the late afternoon chores, Devlin glanced at the time and headed back to his cabin.

He'd felt edgy and off-balance since Chloe's unexpected arrival, though there certainly was no reason for it.

She planned to keep to herself.

He planned to do the same.

In fact, once the rest of the family came home from California, Dev would work on remodeling his cabin—

when he wasn't running and lifting weights—and their paths would rarely cross again.

He collected a .22 Winchester 190 rifle from a padlocked closet and some boxes of ammo from a locked cupboard in his bedroom. The intense, laser-like focus of target practice had never failed to settle his thoughts. After a few hundred rounds or so, he'd definitely have everything back into perspective.

He headed over the rise just beyond his cabin. Below, the ground fell sharply into a broad, grassy meadow rimmed on three sides with a high, curving hillside that created a perfect rifle-range backdrop, while the fourth side opened up into a heavy pine forest leading up into the foothills.

Sure enough, the old wooden target frames were still there, though several were falling into disrepair. He sauntered over, found a dozen old tin cans scattered on the ground nearby and then lined them up on the almost-horizontal crossbar of one of the targets. Then he strode back to a triangular boulder marking a distance of a hundred yards and loaded .22 LRs into the magazine.

It had been almost nine months since he'd felt the weight of an assault rifle in his hands. The simple .22 in his hands had been his grandfather's and felt like a toy in comparison.

But before he could raise it high enough to look through the site and fire, a searing jolt of pain tore through his damaged shoulder.

He winced.

Forced himself to continue.

Struggled to focus.

The shot went wild, pinging off a distant boulder with a puff of dust and rock chips.

One after another were the same, until he'd burned through a hundred rounds and had hit one of the tin cans maybe thirty times, his frustration and anger at himself growing with each pull of the trigger.

He'd refused to believe what the VA docs had told him. He'd been a crack shot—scoring 349 at his last marksmanship qualification—so what did they know?

But lifelong skills and sheer strength of will weren't enough to overcome the truth.

He had just partial vision in his right eye, due to irreparable damage. His shoulder-replacement surgery six months ago had been only a partial fix at best, so it would never be the same.

Was this pathetic performance his future? Or could he regain his strength and skills by July, and qualify for the career he'd been offered?

Maybe it was just a foolish dream, but from now on, he was going to work at it every single day. Weight lifting. Running. Target practice. And he wasn't going to stop until he reached his goal.

A twig snapped. He suddenly sensed that someone was watching. He spun around and froze, scanning the hill behind him, all of his senses on high alert.

But no one was there.

Devlin stopped at the main house, let himself in through the back door and unlocked the pet door so the twins' puppy could go out into the fenced yard at will.

Even with a half-grown pup chasing around the kitchen after a tennis ball, the house felt empty with everyone gone.

He'd arrived late Sunday night, and during the first two days he'd been here, he'd discovered that the little blonde twins seemed to be everywhere all at once, playing with their rascal of a puppy. Building forts with blankets. Trying to be "good helpers" when Grandma Betty or Abby—who had been hired as their nanny and who was now Jess's fiancée—were trying to make a meal. Which meant a lot more spills in the process, though no one seemed to mind the extra mess.

There was so much more laughter in the house now— nothing like the grim silence Devlin and his brothers experienced while growing up. Even with Grandma Betty's best efforts to make it a happier home after Heather's death and Mom's passing the next year, it had felt as if the life had been drained from the house and everyone in it.

Devlin looked in the fridge and found a 9" x 13" pan on the middle shelf, read the directions on the sticky note affixed to the foil wrap and snorted.

Reheat at 350 degrees for 45 minutes. Don't worry about pre-heating the oven. Frozen microwave-ready bags of veggies in freezer. Coconut cake on the counter. Tell Chloe to come to the house for supper. She's had a long trip today. J

Betty had added Chloe's cell number in larger print and underlined it twice, apparently guessing that Devlin might not follow through.

He sighed as he turned on the oven and shoved the pan inside, imagining a meal with Chloe across the table, chattering away. Maybe he could just ignore the note…

Nope.

He'd been career military; as tough, hardened and relentless as any of his buddies. But he still didn't dare ignore his grandma's orders. She'd always loved Dev and his brothers to pieces, but she'd also instilled in them a deep sense of respect and responsibility.

If he failed to be thoughtful, just the disappointment in her voice would make him regret it.

He dutifully made the call on his amplified cell phone, though when Chloe politely declined, he breathed a sigh of relief and said he'd drop off some dinner on his way up to his own cabin, anyhow.

Just as he was pulling the casserole out of the oven, he heard a loud knock on the back door and Chloe let herself inside. "I figured I'd save you the bother and just come down."

She gave a startled laugh as the pup raced over to her and collapsed at her feet, a mass of waving paws and wagging tail. She bent down to rub his fat belly.

She looked up at Devlin, her head cocked. "What is he? Some golden retriever mix, I'd say."

"I've been told his mom was a golden, father unknown."

"What's his name?"

Devlin shot a quick, pained glance at her over his shoulder as he settled the hot casserole on a trivet. Then he turned back to face her so he could read her lips as she spoke. "Uh… Poofy. Thanks to the twins."

"Not exactly the name of a hardworking ranch dog, but he's such a big fluff ball that I can see why." Chloe laughed. "Do the twins belong to Jess?"

He hesitated, debating over how much to say. "He adopted them this past winter. Their mom is Lindsey, our youngest cousin. She…well, she just couldn't handle raising them."

He searched the freezer for frozen vegetables and

held up microwavable bags of corn and green beans. "Preference?"

"Either."

He tossed the green beans into the microwave and pushed the buttons for about four minutes.

When he turned around again, Chloe was staring at him, and he realized that she'd finally seen the scars.

Multiple operations had repaired much of the visible damage, leaving a jagged scar that trailed from his right temple to the corner of his jaw, but as it descended along his neck and into the collar of his shirt, the scarring was heavier.

At least his shirt covered the worst: the twisted, gnarled flesh that draped over his shoulder replacement and upper arm, where much of the bicep muscle was gone forever.

"Devlin." She rose slowly and moved closer, lifting a hand to cradle the side of his face. "What happened?"

He jerked away, resenting the pity in her voice. Alarmed at the unexpected warmth that flowed through him at the touch of her hand.

He didn't talk about the details with anyone. Not the shrink back at the VA hospital, not his docs. And here in Montana, he certainly wouldn't be talking to Jess or Abby or anyone else. However ugly, his scars were nothing compared to the ultimate sacrifice paid by his closest buddies—and he didn't talk about that, either.

It did no good to dredge up the day when three of them were killed in an ambush and he was the only one to walk away. It only fed the nightmares and the guilt, and stirred feelings of desperation because he knew the past could never change.

He silently pulled the green beans from the microwave and dumped them into a serving bowl, then grabbed a couple of plates from the cupboard and gave her one. "Help yourself. I've no idea what's in the casserole."

Clearly ill at ease after his rebuff, she avoided looking at him as he pulled a metal spatula from a crock on the counter that held serving utensils and handed it to her. "The casserole looks wonderful. Ham and scalloped potatoes, I think. Thanks."

He gave her a plate and waited until she served herself, then scooped ample portions onto his own. The tantalizing aroma of this simple home-cooked meal flooded his senses. When had he eaten anything that smelled this good?

Chloe lingered uncertainly by the round oak table in the kitchen, as if debating whether to stay or go. An awkward moment lengthened between them.

"Well," she said finally, "I got a late start from Minneapolis yesterday, so I had to drive the final seven hundred miles today. If you don't mind, I'll take this back to my cabin and return the plate in the morning. I need to settle in and get to work."

With a little wave of her fingers, she let herself out the door.

Work at what? What could she possibly plan to work on in a cabin, in the middle of nowhere?

And for that matter, where had she been all these years? What made her come so far out West when there must have been endless places to stay that were much closer to Minneapolis?

His curiosity about her life was growing.

Poofy followed her for a few steps, then looked back at Devlin, his tail drooping.

He looked down at the crestfallen dog. "Yeah. Lucky it's just you and not Abby or Betty here. I'm sure they'd have something to say about my manners."

Chloe had apparently grown up in more ways than one.

As a kid, Ms. Perpetual Questions had been relentlessly persistent, but she'd clearly gotten the hint and was tactfully planning to give him all the space he wanted.

So maybe he had his peace and quiet back...yet from the strange wrenching in his heart, maybe that wasn't what he wanted after all.

Or was it?

Chapter Two

Well, that had certainly been awkward and embarrassing. But not unexpected as far as Devlin's attitude was concerned, so at least he was still consistent.

If Chloe had known that he was going to be here, she would've given up her dream of three months of perfect, uninterrupted seclusion on this middle-of-nowhere ranch in Montana and headed straight to her new job in Kansas City that she didn't want, but couldn't refuse.

Lifting yet another heavy cardboard box from the trunk of her car, she shouldered her computer bag and started up the rocky trail to her cabin for the fifth time.

At the sound of footsteps behind her, she hesitated for a split second, then kept walking. But she was no match for Devlin's long stride.

"I can carry that box," he said as he fell in beside her. "I'm heading up that direction anyway."

"No need." She sidestepped when he tried to take it.

He gave a low sound of exasperation. "Still independent. I guess you haven't changed that much after all."

Adjusting the awkward weight of the box in her arms, she shot a side glance at him. "Neither have you."

But that wasn't exactly true.

He hadn't been this polite the last time she'd seen him. Or this tall, well-muscled and flat-out handsome.

Back then, he'd been a tall, gangly sixteen-year-old, with a shock of unruly dark hair and the most beautiful silver-blue eyes she'd ever seen—back then, or since. She'd been just eleven, her last summer here, and he'd been her first big, hopeless crush. His lethal combination of teen-idol looks and bad-boy charisma had the girls in town following him like a flock of besotted groupies.

She'd teased him about them just to see his cheeks go red, but she had no doubt that the local women were going to be mighty pleased to see him back on their home turf. If someone, somewhere, wasn't already wearing his ring and planning wedding bells, it wouldn't take long for one of the locals to nab him. And the sooner, the better, before he broke any more hearts.

He certainly wouldn't be breaking hers.

As a child, she'd been his persistent shadow, but in return he'd relentlessly teased her. Only when no one was watching did she ever let herself cry. She understood his behavior now, from an adult perspective. What teenage boy wanted a little girl to be his ever-present tagalong? But the teasing had hurt. He'd made her feel self-conscious and unworthy, and she'd grown to hate her freckles and everything else about herself.

But far worse, he'd hung out with the bad boys in high school—wild parties, lots of booze. She knew it was true—she'd seen him out in the woods and behind the barns, drinking with that rowdy crowd. And that scared her to death.

With a dad like hers, even at eleven she'd known Devlin's drinking was a terrible red flag—a lifetime, ironclad deal-breaker, no questions asked.

No matter how handsome or polite or charming he might be now, she was not looking for romance any longer, and *especially* not with someone who partied and got drunk with his friends.

At the cabin, he stepped in front of her to open the door wide.

"Well, have a good…" He stared at the pile of boxes in the middle of the floor and the mountain of grocery sacks on the counter. "You sure pack light."

At the brief deepening of the laugh lines at the corners of his eyes, she felt the impact of his old charm clear down to her toes. The local women weren't going to be just *pleased* at his return; they were going to be over-the-moon ecstatic.

"*How* long did you say you're staying?"

Dropping the last box onto the stack, she pulled her laptop-case strap from her shoulder and laid the case on the kitchen table. "Three months. I had just enough money saved to stay here that long before I move on."

"What sort of work did you do?"

"I was a secretary for…" she faltered, debating how much to reveal. "…a big investment firm, while putting myself through graduate school."

That much was true, just not entirely complete. And it wasn't like she was a criminal on the run—she'd been exonerated, after all. Even so, she'd already seen the expressions of doubt and accusation on the faces of acquaintances…people who'd *wanted* to believe the worst.

But Devlin had no interest in her. He surely wouldn't think to try googling her on the internet, so it should be possible to simply keep her troubled past where it belonged. In the past.

He eyed her curiously. "What was your major?"

Mom had declared she was foolish to chase dreams that might never come true. When her own mother didn't believe in her, was it ridiculous to think she could ever succeed? Would Devlin laugh if she told him about what she was doing?

"My major was Creative Writing," she said. "That's why I wanted to come out here. I wanted a peaceful, beautiful place to stay, where I could concentrate on my writing with no interruptions. Since I have such happy memories of Montana, this ranch seemed perfect."

"And then where will you go?"

That was the hard part. Knowing Chloe's situation, her sister had offered her a generous salary, and a chance for a fresh start. Far too generous an offer to refuse. But the thought of her future weighed on her shoulders like a mantle of iron.

She might not ever make much money with her writing, so she could hardly afford to turn down Jane's offer, considering her legal debts. But it was the last thing she wanted to do. "I've got a property-management job waiting for me in Kansas City."

He regarded her for a long moment. "You don't exactly look thrilled about it."

"It will be a blessing," she said firmly. "I'll need a job as soon as I leave. But until then, I will count myself fortunate to stay here once again."

He seemed to consider that for a while, then sighed. "I expect Betty will be happy to see you."

Chloe couldn't help but smile at his less-than-gracious attitude. "I can't wait to see her, either. After my mom took off, I used to pretend that she was my grandma. She still sends me birthday cards with invitations to come visit, but this is my first time back. When will the family be home?"

He was bent over the dead bolt on the door, checking it out. He didn't answer.

He'd ignored some of her questions, and twice he hadn't responded when she called out his name. She'd figured he was just being his usual distant self.

But now she wondered. Devlin had been physically wounded and probably had deeper, more-emotional wounds, as well. Who wouldn't with all of the dangers he'd probably faced in battle?

Had he also ended up with hearing damage due to his military career?

It was entirely plausible, but prying personal information from him had always been a futile task. She waited until he looked up again. "When will the rest of your family be back?"

"A week from tomorrow."

Sure enough, now she could see that he wasn't just listening; he was trying to *watch* her speak. "Aren't the twins in school?"

"Kindergarten, but they're on spring break." A corner of his mouth lifted in a fleeting, affectionate grin at the mention of the little girls. "They seemed pretty excited about Disneyland."

"I can believe it. They'll sure have a lot of days with Mickey."

Devlin shrugged. "Not all of that time. They're visiting their mom in San Diego, Jess is looking at some stallion prospects and Abby will be checking out a few colleges."

"Who is Abby?"

"She was hired as a nanny last fall, and now she and Jess are engaged."

"But she's looking at colleges, so she's leaving?"

"Considering online programs, I guess."

"Good for her." Chloe slid a knife through the shipping tape on the top of a cardboard box labeled Kitchenware and inspected the contents. *Books.*

She straightened and rested a hand at the small of her back. "You'll have eight busy days 'til they get back, then. Are there ranch hands to do the chores?"

"Nope. I told Jess I could do it. Might as well earn my keep while I'm here." He touched the brim of his Stetson and gave her a slight nod of farewell, then turned for the door. "'Night."

She'd already seen how he favored his weak right arm and shoulder, while handling that heavy pan of ham and scalloped potatoes. And when she'd heard the sound of gunfire down in the shooting range this afternoon, she'd walked up the hill and briefly watched him struggle to hit the targets.

At sixteen he wouldn't have missed a single shot. But even from the top of the hill, she'd seen his rifle barrel wobble. Not wanting to embarrass him, she'd slipped away before he noticed she was there, but the problem was clear enough. How was he was going to manage doing chores?

Maybe he wasn't warm and friendly, and he certainly wouldn't ever be a pal. But she just couldn't ignore someone in need, even if he wished she would disappear.

"Hey, Devlin—if you need any help, just holler," she called out. "You've got my cell number, now."

He didn't respond.

She stared at the door closing behind him, feeling an old, familiar wave of compassion and frustration.

He hadn't wanted help or sympathy years ago, and he clearly didn't want it now. Which was fine. She already had a lot on her plate without trying to get past his prickly defenses.

Still, a warm sense of hope and purpose spread through her. She'd volunteered at the local no-kill animal shelter over the past few years and had rehabbed many foster animals in her little rental house. Wounded birds. Abused dogs. Feral cats. With love and care, she'd been able to send all of them back to the shelter when they were ready to find good forever homes.

Granted, a man like Devlin was a lot more complex than, say, a Corgi, but could she help *him*?

As a cheerleader and a compassionate listener, maybe she could tactfully help him somehow…or push him to find the services and support he needed. If only he would let her.

She re-taped the box she'd just opened, set it aside and sliced the shipping tape on a box marked Linens. This one was stuffed with sweaters. She sat back in her heels with a sigh.

Obviously her hasty departure from Minneapolis hadn't been conducive to good organization, but she'd been so careful otherwise.

She'd avoided mentioning her moving plans to the few friends she had left. Canceled her newspaper and magazine subscriptions. Switched her bills to online payments. And then she'd arranged a three-month disappearance at a private Montana ranch, where she would pay for everything in cash.

Escaping that one persistent reporter—who had continued to paint her in his series of articles as a greedy, conniving Jezebel angling for a wealthy, married man—had been her first priority, and speed had been her greater concern.

Even after she'd been exonerated, the reporter had

refused to let the story go. Since then she had applied for several jobs. Every time, the interviewer had looked at her name, then looked up at her face with dawning recognition. And that job possibility had ended.

But now she was far away. Starting her life over. And hopefully he'd find no trail to follow.

Devlin groaned as he watched the twins' pony hightail it out of the front of the barn. For an animal that fat and lazy, Lollipops showed surprising speed now that he was free.

He'd turned his back on the beast for a split second while dropping hay into the corner manger of the pony's stall, never expecting that Lollipops would move a muscle except to head towards his grain and hay. He'd seen the twins riding in the arena, trying to get the pony into a lope, and a truck with an empty gas tank moved faster.

Muttering under his breath, he grabbed a bucket of pellets, plus a halter and lead rope, and jogged outside to the parking area.

The pony was nowhere in sight.

Not by the pasture fence to the east of the barn, where a couple dozen broodmares close to their foaling dates could be seen standing slant-hipped around three round bale feeders, whiling away their time until being brought in for the night.

Not along the fence on the other side of the barn, where a dozen mares and their new foals were out on forty acres of pasture.

And not along the fence line perpendicular to the broodmare pasture, farther to the west, where a herd of heavily pregnant cows were lined up along the long feed bunk.

That meant the pony could be heading down the long

gravel lane toward the highway, which would be a remarkably bad idea given the semitrucks that blew by a good twenty miles an hour over the speed limit. Or, if he'd thundered past the broodmare pasture, he might have turned into the dirt lane leading up to the summer range pastures. Though unlikely that he'd leave close proximity to the other horses, he could end up lost forever if he skirted the fences and kept going.

Devlin needed help, and Chloe was the last person he'd want to call, but she was also the only other person here. So be it. She could always say no. He reached for his phone—and realized he'd left it in his cabin when he'd gone back for some more Tylenol.

At the abrupt sound of the pup barking excitedly, Devlin heaved a sigh of relief and jogged up to the main house. *Bingo.*

Repeatedly jumping up against the chain-link fence surrounding the yard, Poofy wagged his tail furiously when Devlin came into view. Then he ran to the far corner and began barking anew, his attention fixed on the trail leading to the cabins.

Which wasn't exactly good news, either.

The final cabin sat atop the hill, looking over a series of rising foothills that led up into the mountains and the unfenced government land that abutted a corner of the Langford ranch.

Devin weighed the options of going back to saddle a horse, grabbing a four-wheeler from the machine shed or just continuing on foot to the top of the hill. His cabin overlooked a grassy meadow on the other side of the hill, already green with tender spring grass. Surely the greedy little beast wouldn't go farther than that.

What on earth would he say to the girls if he'd lost their pony forever? Mountain lions, bears and even the occasional wolf were all possible out here. And all would consider a chubby, elderly pony easy prey.

He hesitated, then knocked on Chloe's door, softly first, then louder. From inside he could hear a radio. Was she just ignoring him? Putting him in his place? Swallowing his pride for the sake of the twins and their beloved pony, he banged on the door louder.

No answer.

So be it. He headed back up the trail, hoping Lollipops didn't prove to be too cagey for one person to catch.

Just past his cabin, Devin shielded the sun from his eyes with his hand and muttered a rusty prayer as he searched the makeshift rifle range in the meadow and the surrounding timber. Nothing.

Wait...

At the far side of the meadow, something was rustling through the underbrush. A moment later the vagabond pony stepped out of the shadows with a slender figure at his side.

Chloe.

Relief and gratitude flooded through him. *Thank you, Lord.*

His boots sent pebbles skittering down the rocky slope as he descended the steep hill to meet them. Sunlight filtering through the pine branches turned the palomino pony's coat to molten gold, and picked out the gold and ruby highlights of Chloe's auburn hair. If he had any artistic abilities, he would've wanted to capture the beauty of the scene on canvas.

Her arrival at the ranch had been the last thing he'd expected. He'd resolved to keep his distance from her. But right now he couldn't think of a more welcome sight.

"Looking for someone?" Chloe called out as they

met in the middle of the grassy meadow. She was holding on to a narrow leather belt she'd buckled around the pony's neck. "He was really trucking when he ran past my cabin, but he wasn't hard to catch once I caught up with him."

"Thanks, Chloe."

"He melted at the sight of a carrot. I think he was having second thoughts about missing his dinner."

"From the looks of him, he hasn't missed many." Devlin slipped the halter onto him and gave Chloe her belt back. "I owe you one. You've made the twins very happy."

She said something he couldn't hear, so he looked over at her to watch her lips as she spoke. "What?"

"Who is this little guy, by the way?" she repeated.

Dev started leading the pony toward home, with Chloe on his other side. Only then did he notice two remaining carrots still sticking up from the back pocket of her jeans. "His name is Lollipops."

She laughed. "I'll have to say, those girls are certainly original."

At the top of the hill, Devlin stopped in front of his cabin. "Hang on to him a minute, would you? I need to grab my cell phone."

When he came out with his phone, Chloe was cradling the pony's head in the crook of her arm, his thick, long white mane flowing over her arm like a waterfall. The tender pose and the soft glow of her beautiful complexion nudged at his heart, and once again he wished he could capture the scene with oils or watercolors.

"So, is this where you live?" she asked, staring up at the dilapidated cabin. "In *that*?"

He nodded. "For now."

"It looks…rustic," she said tactfully. "Is it better inside?"

He snorted. "Nope."

"If I hadn't shown up, then you'd be in the nicer cabin, right?" She bit her lower lip. "I'm sorry—though not quite sorry enough to switch. This one is scary."

After some of the places he'd been in the Middle East, it was a palace. "It'll do."

"I could break down that door with a sneeze. Does it even lock?"

"Not yet."

She raised her gaze to the mossy, swaybacked roof. "And does it leak?"

"I'm sure it does, given the water stains on the floor. But it hasn't rained since I got here, so I'm good."

"So far." She rolled her eyes. "I'd guess varmints moved inside long ago. Right?"

"Just the mice and chipmunks that aren't giving up their territory without a fight. I need to borrow a barn cat from the horse barn."

She visibly shuddered. "Really, this cabin would make a nice bonfire. Then a new one could be built in its place. Why did Jess give you this sorry mess? Even a corner in the horse barn would be better. Maybe the tack room?"

When she turned away to study the cabin, he could only guess at half of the words she was saying, but he certainly caught her drift.

"Well?" Now she looked exasperated, and a warrior's gleam lit her eyes as she propped her hands on her hips and glared at him. "When Jess gets back, I'm going to talk to him."

This was the Chloe he remembered, ready to go toe-to-toe with anyone, in righteous defense of her latest cause. Usually in *his* defense, to tell the truth, though Dad had never been impressed. He'd told her father to "keep that kid out of my way" more than once.

But Devlin didn't need anyone—especially Chloe— standing up for him now. Especially against a brother who had welcomed him home with open arms, despite how he'd failed the family three years ago. He was the prodigal son…only worse.

"Jess wanted me to stay in the main house, but I prefer my privacy. This works."

"But—"

"And I'm starting renovations on it, so it'll be convenient to stay up here. Once everyone gets home, I'll get to work. Then I'll reno the middle cabin next. I want to get both done before I leave. As…as a favor."

Penance was the right word, but that would open up all sorts of questions he had no intention of answering, and some that he couldn't.

He wondered what Chloe would think if she knew the truth about the kind of man he really was. But then again, maybe she'd known all along.

Chapter Three

With the windows wide-open to the crisp, clean mountain air, Chloe had slept better than she had in years. Funny how she hadn't been back since she was eleven, yet this still seemed like home.

She'd put all of her perishable foods in the fridge as soon as she had arrived yesterday. This morning she'd unpacked her clothes and scrubbed the kitchen cupboards. Then she'd put away the rest of the groceries she'd picked up on her way to the ranch, as well as the more unusual canned and dry items she'd brought from Minneapolis.

Now, with the early-morning sun beaming through the windows, she searched through the stack of cardboard boxes on the floor until she found her electric breadmaker. She then collected the necessary ingredients and opened up the file labeled Experiments in her laptop.

Cinnamon pecan bread. Version 12.

Versions one through six had risen to glorious heights and then stuck to the inside lid of the breadmaker like wet plaster. Seven through eleven had been too dense, collapsed or had the tenderness of shoe leather. But eleven had been *sooo* close.

Who knew it would be so difficult to replicate her late Grandma Lydia's family-famous recipes for modern appliances? At this rate, it was going to take a decade to get everything right.

But then…she smiled as she carefully measured the ingredients into the machine according to her latest notes, this time adding honey instead of brown sugar and adding a tablespoon of vital wheat gluten. Once she'd retested and photographed every recipe, she could finish her final revision of her cookbook manuscript.

While the breadmaker was chugging through its Knead Cycle, she thumbed through the yellowed, tattered index cards under the cookies tab in Lydia's wooden recipe box until she found one bearing Lydia's silent, high praise—so stained and worn that the ink was barely legible.

My Best Chocolate Chip Cookies had to be a keeper, even if it needed tweaking to appeal to modern tastes.

First time through, exactly as written. The following efforts would be when the fun of experimenting began.

The wonderful scents of real butter, vanilla and brown sugar filled the air as she creamed the first ingredients, already hinting that Lydia had been onto something with the exact ratios in this recipe.

By the time Chloe pulled the second cookie sheet out of the oven, she'd polished off two cookies from the first pan and couldn't help but nab a melty-soft treasure from the pan just out of the oven. *Enough.*

She usually tried to be careful about eating sweets, and certainly knew better than to indulge like this. Still…these cookies weren't only wonderful; they felt like a connection to the loving grandmother she'd lost years ago.

She closed her eyes, savoring the rich, perfect confection. Imagining her grandmother measuring the same ingredients, enjoying this same flavor and aroma decades ago.

She opened her eyes with a start. Had she just moaned with pure enjoyment? *Really?*

Then she heard it again. But it wasn't the sound of enjoyment. It was a low, agonized moan, and it was coming from outside the cabin's screen door.

Definitely not human.

Too quiet to be a bear.

For all she knew, Devlin still loved warm cookies, but it would take more imagination than she possessed to envision him with his face pressed against the screen in hopes that she would share. He'd made it more than clear that he planned to keep his distance.

She warily circled the end of the kitchen counter and sidestepped along the wall until she could peek out of the screen door, ready to grab the heavier exterior door, slam it shut and lock the dead bolt against anything big and scary.

But nothing was there.

Just the soft rustling of the pines buffeted by a gentle breeze. A carpet of rusty pine needles and the empty, narrow path leading down to the trail.

Something moaned again, this time a little weaker, filled with pain and hopelessness that grabbed her by the heart. Easing the screen door open a few inches, she scanned the area again and then tentatively stepped outside. A wounded coyote or wolf wasn't anything she dared encounter, but...

Her gaze dropped to the foundation of the cabin and

what looked like a filthy gray pile of rags. A *big* pile at that.

"Oh, my," she whispered. "What happened to you?"

Yesterday had not gone well.

Just the thought of how badly he'd done on the shooting range made Devlin want to slam a fist through a wall, except then he'd have yet another injury, and yet another barrier to having any kind of future at all.

Nothing was going to stand in his way.

The Marines had been his life for ten years. What other skills did he have but those of a warrior? If he didn't qualify for the security-company job in New York, what other career was there for a man like him? None.

So this morning he'd risen early. Even before doing chores, he'd done two reps of the exercises given by his physical therapist. Started lifting weights again to build the strength in his damaged right arm and shoulder. He'd run four miles.

And then he'd gone back to the meadow and burned through another hundred rounds of ammo.

His aim had been even worse and his shoulder joint was still on fire from the stress—too shaky to even hold a cup of coffee by the time he'd finished shooting. His muscles ached.

But he could not afford to give up, and he was determined to complete this same routine every single day until he was as good as the man he'd been before. Or better.

Surprised to see an urgent text from Chloe, Devlin awkwardly unsaddled the two-year-old he was starting to work out in the arena, put him in a stall and drove the four-wheeler up to Chloe's cabin.

Even before coming to a stop, he could smell warm cookies, fresh from the oven, and something else that was rich with cinnamon and butter. Homemade bread?

Almost dizzy from the tantalizing aroma, he took a deep breath and headed for the front steps of the cabin, where Chloe was crouched next to something covered in a fluffy yellow afghan.

"Look at this poor thing," she said, her voice wavering. "Just look at how badly she's hurt."

She edged sideways and pulled back the afghan to reveal a large, gaunt dog covered in matted fur—gray or white, he couldn't tell. One of its front legs appeared badly mangled, but with all of that thick fur crusted with dried blood, dirt and twigs, it was hard to see. Now that it had been uncovered, he detected the foul odor of infection.

"Does she have a collar?" he said in a low voice.

"No. And she's really weak. She needs to get to a vet before it's too late." She looked up at him, her eyes filled with tears. "But my SUV can't make it up the narrow trail and I can't carry her down. Will you help me?"

He hesitated. He'd seen this sort of thing before and knew the dog's chances were slim, given its overall poor condition. The vet bills for this stray could be huge. But like Chloe, he'd never been able to turn away from something—or someone—in need.

Except for his own father and brother, three years ago, and that was a burden of guilt he would never escape.

"I'll bring the four-wheeler up close. Do you have any long pieces of cloth we can use for a muzzle? She's in a lot of pain and might bite when we try to move her."

Chloe nodded and disappeared into the cabin, then returned with a bedsheet covered with pink flowers.

"Don't worry, this sheet didn't come with the cabin. It's one of mine," she explained as she ripped a long strip from it and helped him form a soft figure eight around the dog's nose and the back of her head.

Her fingertips brushed his hand as they fastened the makeshift muzzle, and there it was again—the little flash of warmth and awareness that shot up his arm and landed square in his chest. And from her indrawn breath and the shocked look in her big eyes, she felt it, too. She fumbled at securing the knot, and they had to start all over again.

Bearing most of the weight with his good arm, he helped Chloe ease the dog onto part of the afghan and used it as a sling to lift her into the back cargo area of the four-wheeler. The animal raised her head for a moment and whimpered, then dropped back down and thumped her tail weakly.

On their way down to the hill, Chloe crouched over the dog, trying to hold her steady while Devlin drove slowly around the worst of the rocky bumps, then headed for his own SUV.

"No," Chloe protested. "If you just tell me where the vet clinic is, I can take her. I know you're busy, and anyway this was my idea. My work can wait, and I should take responsibility."

"We can figure that out later." Devlin pulled out his cell phone and googled *Pine Bend veterinarians*, called what appeared to be the only clinic in town these days and then slipped the phone back into his pocket. "They said to bring the dog on in. I'll drive."

"But—"

He set his jaw. "You might need help."

She finally capitulated and helped gently move the dog into the back of his SUV. She gave Devlin a grateful smile. "I'm not sure if I turned off the stove. Can I use the four-wheeler to run up and check?"

He nodded tersely and ran a gentle hand over the dog's quivering flank, then covered her with part of the afghan and shut the tailgate. He got behind the wheel and started the motor.

He'd intended to simply disappear at the Langford ranch for a while, to drop out of sight while physically preparing for what he wanted to do with the rest of his life. A life that would be far different now than what he'd always imagined.

And he'd intended to avoid Pine Bend for however long he stayed.

He could well imagine the small-town gawkers and their avid curiosity over a Langford son returning with obvious injuries from a war far away. Thanks to his father, the Langford name spurred resentment in some and envy in others. There would be stares. Whispers. Intrusive questions. And, of course, the effusive, empty show of sympathy that he recoiled from every single time.

Yet here he was, heading for town. His resolve had lasted all of four days, thanks to Chloe and her compassionate heart. But how could he refuse?

At least he didn't recognize the vet's name, so maybe she was new to town since he'd left home. Maybe she wouldn't even recognize the Langford name.

Chloe was gone and back again in a flash, and when she climbed into the front seat of his SUV, she put a foil-covered paper plate on the console between them and settled a stainless steel tumbler into the cupholder.

"The stove was already off, but while I was there I took my bread out of the breadmaker, and decided I should bring you these as thanks for helping me. Milk and cookies."

The intoxicating aroma of chocolate chip cookies filled the air when she lifted the foil.

She looked up at him with a twinkle in her eyes. "And, I admit, giving these cookies away is a desperate ploy on my part, because I cannot leave them alone."

Taken aback by the thoughtful gesture, his gaze locked on hers and time seemed to stand still. How could someone this pretty still be single?

He snorted under his breath. *That* didn't take much thought. She'd been a persistent little pest when she was younger. If she was anything like that now, prospective boyfriends probably hit the road in record time…

Only, that wasn't really true.

He'd believed it as a callow teenage boy, wrapped up in his own world, with little regard for the child who'd looked up to him like some hero.

The truth was that she'd been sweet and thoughtful as a little girl, and she was just as sweet and thoughtful now. And pretty. *Really* pretty. The kind of woman who made a man look twice, catch his breath and then think about a lifetime commitment.

So why was she here alone, instead of raising a family of pretty little redheads somewhere, with an adoring husband at her side?

He cleared his throat and turned the key in the ignition, forcing his attention to the ranch lane ahead and then the highway into town. *Not his business.*

He'd be leaving the ranch by July, she'd be leaving even sooner. There was no sense in thinking about anything beyond basic courtesy.

But he was already sure that he wouldn't stop thinking about her anytime soon, and he definitely wouldn't stop thinking about those cookies. He'd finished every last one by the time they were halfway into town, and he still wanted more. "Thanks. They were awesome."

She chuckled softly. "It's my Grandma Lydia's recipe, so I can't take any credit."

He sorted through his old memories. "I think I remember her visiting here. She used sign language, right?"

Chloe nodded. "Mom started teaching me sign when I was a toddler so I could talk to her, but Grandma passed away when I was eight. I barely knew her, sad to say."

Devlin glanced in the rearview mirror and adjusted the angle to check on the dog in the back. The poor thing hadn't done so much as whimper during the fifteen-mile trip to Pine Bend. Was she even still alive? Given the extent of the wounds and obvious infection, she was going to face a long recovery if she even made it into town.

At the clinic, two vet techs came out and helped carry the dog into an exam room. The older one, a woman in her fifties with Bonnie on her name tag, began an initial exam, while the younger gal filled out information on a clipboard.

When the younger tech left to get a handheld chip scanner, Bonnie cocked her head and gave Devlin a long look. "You must be Gus Langford's middle son. Am I right?"

Since he'd given his name over the phone before driving into town, her guess wasn't much of a stretch, but he knew a conversational ploy when he heard it, and also knew how to deflect. He nodded curtly.

"Sorry about your dad, bless his soul. Parkinson's is such a cruel disease. He had a long, hard struggle, but Betty and Jess did right by him." She nodded, as if agreeing with herself. "You should have no doubt about that."

If there was any accusation in her voice, he couldn't hear it, but he felt a sliver of guilt at any rate. He should have been here. He *could* have been here at least part of the time, to help out at the ranch. But he'd let the pain and bitterness of the past inform his decisions, and death offered no second chances.

The other tech bustled into the room to scan the dog for any identification chips, and the young vet—Dr. Weldon, according to her name badge—walked into the room ten minutes later.

"My goodness," she said softly. "Who do you have here?"

"She was laying outside my cabin," Chloe said. "I don't know how she managed to get there, because she's so weak."

The vet gently examined the dog and shook her head. "Obviously she's had this injury for some time, and that infection doesn't look good. With her high fever and malaise, it could well be systemic by now."

"But you can save her, right?" Chloe pleaded. "The poor thing deserves a chance."

"Once we've got her cleaned up better, get some X-rays and bloodwork drawn, we'll have a better idea of what we're dealing with. Why don't you two step out for a bit—we won't be long."

When they all convened in the exam room once more, the vet ran a gentle hand over the dog's ribs. "She does have oblique fractures of the second through fifth metacarpals."

Devlin frowned. "*Four* bones? That doesn't sound good."

"Think of them like the bones that lie close together

within the palm of your hand. They do show less displacement than I feared, so that's in her favor. At first glance, I was expecting comminuted—badly shattered—fractures that were perhaps beyond repair, with significant soft tissue damage and possibly the start of necrosis. Meaning, her best chance would be amputation of that leg."

Chloe drew in a sharp breath, and the vet looked up at her with a gentle smile. "You'd be surprised at how well dogs can do on three legs."

"She has a good chance of recovery, then?"

The vet nodded. "She's dehydrated and hasn't eaten in a long while, so I want to debride her wounds, start IV fluids and antibiotics, and put her on a critical nutrition diet. She does need surgical repair of that leg, probably with bone plates and screws. Do you have any idea where she might have come from?"

Devlin cleared his throat. "No idea. I've been away from Montana for a long time, so I don't know the locals anymore."

"With no chip and no collar, we can't contact her owners." Dr. Weldon studied the dog for a moment. "I wonder if this could be Leonard Farley's dog." She looked up at the older tech, who shrugged. "Farley was an old Vietnam vet who lived by himself in a remote area. Hikers found him dead last fall. Heart attack, according to the autopsy. There were no relatives to contact, but the sheriff told me he owned a Great Pyrenees service dog that no one ever found."

"From the looks of her, this dog didn't have much more time left." Devlin shook his head slowly, imagining the dog's struggle to survive on its own for so long—even throughout an entire Montana winter. "After what she's been through, she deserves good care and a good home. I'll take responsibility for now. If an owner turns up, he can settle with me later."

"No—I will," Chloe said firmly. "You were kind enough to help me with getting her here, but it isn't fair to let you pick up the bills."

Chloe and her foolish pride. Yet he could hardly fault her for her strong sense of honor, and his respect for her grew.

Dr. Weldon looked between the two of them with a wry smile. "Usually I've got people trying to *avoid* responsibility in these cases. I'll put you both down and let you figure it out between the two of you later."

"Just give it to me." Chloe had that stubborn gleam in her eyes again, but this time she wasn't going to win.

A whopping vet bill could be devastating to someone like her, who was between jobs and driving a battered fifteen-year-old SUV. And knowing her parents, they probably came to her for money rather than the other way around. She wouldn't have any help from them.

For all the mistakes he'd made during his life in Montana, for all the times he'd hardened his heart and resolutely gone his own way without looking back, this could be one small chance to finally do the right thing.

Chapter Four

Chloe had tried to beat him to it, but Devlin had waved her away and insisted that the receptionist run only his credit card against the mounting veterinary expenses for the dog.

His generosity still surprised her.

It wasn't like he'd been particularly friendly since she'd arrived, and even now, during the endless, silent drive back to the ranch, he'd kept his gaze riveted to the road ahead and hadn't said a word. Was he angry? Upset? Fed up?

His stoic expression revealed nothing about his thoughts, and by the time they pulled to a stop in front of the horse barn, she couldn't wait to climb out of the vehicle and escape to the solitude of her cabin.

"Thanks," she murmured. "I appreciate everything you did."

He pulled the key from the ignition without looking at her, and she belatedly realized that she'd forgotten to raise her voice. Since discovering that he didn't hear well, she'd made sure to speak louder and stand closer if she had anything to say.

"Thank you," she repeated.

He glanced over at her as he unbuckled his seat belt. "No problem."

She bit her lower lip. "You stopped whatever you were doing to help me with the dog. Were you doing chores? Can I help you to return the favor?"

He shook his head as he got out of the truck.

"Please?" She'd seen him wince when they lifted the injured dog onto the back of the four-wheeler, and again when they'd moved her into the SUV. None of the ranch chores could be easy for him.

"Thanks, but no." A muscle along the side of his jaw twitched when he glanced at the time on the home screen of his cell phone. He started striding to the horse barn. "I have six two-year-olds to ride. I'll do chores later."

With his damaged shoulder, swinging a heavy saddle pad into perfect position, followed by the awkward weight of a thirty-five-to-forty-pound saddle, could not be easy.

She jogged to catch up so he could hear her. "Perfect! I can help with that. While you're riding, I can saddle the next horse, so you don't need to do that. And I can unsaddle and take care of each one as you finish. It'll go much faster for you, right?"

He muttered something unintelligible under his breath that did not sound like an agreement.

"Or," she added brightly, "I imagine Jess left written instructions for the chores. So I could start on those instead. Your choice."

He stopped so abruptly in front of the barn that she nearly ran into him. He automatically reached out with both hands to steady her shoulders. A rush of warmth sped through her at his touch and she felt a blush climbing to her cheeks.

He quickly released her and stepped back, as if he'd touched something hot. Had he felt it, too?

"Look, Chloe. I know you want to be helpful. But I don't *need*…" He looked down into her face. His shoulder slumped in defeat. "Suit yourself. There's a clipboard hanging in the feed room. The stalls have automatic waterers, but the horses need their feed pellets, supplements and hay *exactly* according to the list. And go ahead and feed the broodmares, too—the last twelve stalls at the end of the aisle—but I'll bring them inside later. Any questions?"

"Got it." She beamed up at him, though the long-suffering, patient tone in his voice made her remember the old days, when she was just a kid and might have kicked him in the knee in response. She was certainly no novice when it came to ranch life.

She'd spent every spare minute out in these barns, helping her dad. Playing with the dogs and cats. Riding the well-broken babysitter horses the Langford boys had outgrown. During her last summer here, she'd started going along to the horse shows, to help her dad get the horses ready for halter and performance classes. She'd even worked the western pleasure horses in the practice arena before their classes, so they'd be quiet and steady.

It hadn't been a perfect life—not with her bickering parents and the drinking her dad had tried to hide. But it had been a *good* life, and she'd never stopped missing the wide-open skies of Montana ranch country and the joy of riding to her heart's content.

Humming under her breath, she headed for the feed room and got to work.

Devlin dropped the two-year-old buckskin mare into a walk, shook some slack in the reins and circled the arena a half dozen times. After he headed her into the center of the indoor arena, he eased her into a side pass to the left, and then the right, before backing her up across the arena.

Like the other three horses he'd ridden today, she was calm and smooth, with a low headset and easy manners. Jess had obviously been doing a great job with them all.

At least the mare had worked well. Today he felt like an old man pushing 110 years old. He dismounted slowly, mindful of his aching muscles and sore joints from his earlier workout with weights, physical therapy exercises and a long run. He stroked the mare's neck, then led her into the horse barn, where he unbridled her, slipped on her halter and crosstied her in front of the tack room.

"Great job with her," Chloe exclaimed as she stepped from the tack room and into the barn aisle. "I didn't want to bother you, so I watched for a bit through the picture window in there. You still ride like you never spent a day away from the ranch."

"Thanks." He'd spent more time on horseback than on his own two feet from the time he could walk, but it had been well over ten years since he'd been on a horse, and his muscles were letting him know it. Not that he would ever admit it to her.

He unsaddled the mare, taking most of the weight of the saddle in his left arm, but Chloe took it from him and settled it on a saddle stand in the aisle, to be used on the next horse.

"How many horses do you have left to ride?"

"Two." He tipped his head toward the two stalls on his left.

He reached for a brush, but she nabbed it first. "I

still feel like I owe you some time. Let me take care of this mare, or I can get the next one ready. Your choice."

"Really, I—"

She lifted a shoulder in a faint shrug, her eyes twinkling, and he suddenly couldn't look away.

He'd never noticed, when she was just a kid, but her eyes were the exact shade of his late mother's blue topaz ring, the one that had entranced him when he was young. Held in a sunbeam, it could send showers of diamonds dancing across a room.

The memory tugged at his heart.

"The buckskin, it is," she announced, pulling him away from his memories. "Take the help while you can get it, cowboy. After this I'll be working in my cabin 24/7."

He watched her start brushing the mare, the silver bracelets on her wrist sparkling under the bright fluorescent lights overhead, and then he headed down the aisle to bring a paint gelding out to a second set of crossties.

The gelding threw his head high in the air and danced sideways, the whites of his eyes and his swiveling ears telegraphing his fear when Devlin hooked the crosstie snaps to his halter.

"Someone hasn't been so good to you, have they, buddy," he murmured as he began brushing the animal's quivering hide.

He moved slowly and easily, talking to him nonstop. But when it came time to settle the saddle pad in place, the colt cringed as far away as he could.

Devlin resorted to sliding the saddle pad along the colt's neck, flanks and hindquarters, and then did the same on the other side until the colt realized it wasn't going to attack him and settled down.

Chloe came over to stand by the gelding's head and stroked his sleek neck. "Has this guy been saddled before?"

"The owners said he'd been ridden a half dozen times. If that's true, I'd hate to see how it was done. Pretty rough, I'd guess." Devlin slid the saddle pad into place, then draped the cinch and flank strap over the seat of the saddle before lifting it high and gently lowering it into position. "They nicknamed him Crazy Pants, but I'm guessing that attitude isn't his fault."

She idly rubbed behind the horse's ears now, and he'd dropped his head lower to rest his chin on her shoulder. "Has he been here long?"

Devlin glanced at her. "His owners dropped him off two days ago. I long-lined him in the arena for thirty minutes before saddling him yesterday, and just took it slow."

"My guess is that some local know-it-all said he could break a horse fast and cheap, like some old-time, bronco-busting cowboy. What a mistake. It just means that a good trainer has to work harder to undo all of that harm."

"My thoughts, exactly." Devlin lightly snugged up the cinch, letting the gelding relax before tightening it up a little more.

When had he last stood around talking about ranch work and horses? Not since he'd taken off in a hot, furious rush to join the Marines at nineteen, probably. He hadn't missed all of this when he'd been away. He'd been *relieved* to be gone, away from the anger and tension and impossible expectations this ranch represented.

Yet strangely enough, some old memories—the *better* ones—were starting to sift into his thoughts, and it almost felt good to be back. And who would've thought he'd ever find any point of agreement—much less feel such a connection—to his old childhood nemesis?

He shoved those thoughts away.

He had no plans to stay forever, no plans to stir up old relationships or find anything new. Montana was only a brief stop on his way to a new future, if only he knew what that should be.

Chloe gave him an uncertain smile, as if she knew exactly what he was thinking. "I'll just put the buckskin in her stall, then. Can I saddle your last horse before I go?"

"No," Devlin said, a little too sharply. "Uh…no thanks"

"Accepting a simple favor doesn't mean you'll be shackled into some big commitment, Dev." She rolled her eyes. "Believe me, there's absolutely no risk of that. But take my advice—you might want to start resurrecting your social skills. As a civilian, you're really gonna need 'em."

Taken aback, he watched as she turned on her heel and strode out of the barn door. A burst of laughter rose from somewhere deep in his chest that he couldn't hold back.

His pesky little shadow of old had certainly grown up since she'd left the ranch all those years ago, and she'd just neatly put him in his place.

The more he saw her, the more she intrigued him and the more he wanted… But what did he want exactly? An evening of dinner and dancing, and hours of conversation over a candlelit table? The chance to run his hands through that beautiful long mane of rich auburn hair? The chance to hold her in his arms and never let her go?

It was nothing that he could even think about right now. He couldn't afford to be sidetracked, and he should be relieved that she was flat-out not interested in him, because that would make their mutual time here at the ranch far easier.

But was that what he really wanted?

Chapter Five

Of all the nerve.

Pretty sure that steam might start coming from her ears at any moment, Chloe grabbed the baking soda, measured out two teaspoons and dumped them into the mixing bowl.

She'd felt she owed Devlin a debt of gratitude, so she'd tried to be helpful and make his day a little easier when they got back from the vet clinic yesterday.

Yet when he finally gave in and let her do the chores, he'd made it seem as if he was doing *her* a favor—and he'd even seemed edgy about it. Like he thought she was setting her sights on him or something. *As if.*

And when she'd finally made it clear that—unlike all the other women who probably flocked to his side— she was not the least bit interested, he'd had the audacity to laugh.

Granted, he'd waited until she was out of the barn, but his short burst of laughter had followed her as she headed toward the trail leading to the cabins. Fortunately he wasn't around to see her cheeks burn bright with mortification.

It had been eighteen years since she'd lived on this

ranch. *Eighteen years* since she was a little girl who followed him around like a devoted puppy, and in the interim she'd graduated from college. Gone back for her master's degree, held a steady job. Granted, that last little detail of her life had gone terribly wrong, but she was certainly a grown, independent woman.

And yet the dynamic between them was no different than when she was eleven.

Resting her palms on the countertop, she took a deep breath, studied her grandmother's recipe for chocolate cake once more and then groaned as she caught her latest error. She dumped the contents of the mixing bowl in the trash.

Second try, second time she'd mixed up teaspoons and tablespoons or grabbed the wrong ingredient. At this rate she would need to make that fifteen-mile trip into Pine Bend by tomorrow, and hopefully the little grocery store would have everything she needed.

Her cell phone announced a text message with a chime.

Sidestepping along the counter, she tapped the screen. Devlin.

Vet called. Dog had surgery this morning. Doing fine. Said we can stop in at clinic to see her. Wants her there until at least Monday or Tuesday.

The good news erased her frustration. She thought for a moment, then texted back.

I need some things in town anyway, so I'll stop in to see her today.

She started her recipe over. *Thank you, Lord*, she thought as she creamed the room-temperature butter and sugar. That poor dog deserved a good life after all she had been through, and Chloe was going to give her that loving forever home.

Today was Friday. She counted up the days until Tuesday, trying to guess just how much the vet bill would be, then realized she didn't want to know. Not yet. But whatever it was, she would pay Devlin back, once she started her job in Kansas City.

Her phone chimed again.

I'm heading for the feed store in town. You can come along if you'd like. I'll go to the vet clinic first.

Practicality warred with her pride as she turned the mixer on high. She really did want to see how the dog was doing. But the thirty-mile round trip meant more gas and more miles on her old SUV. Was it worth spending that money just to avoid another awkward encounter with Devlin?

Her bruised heart said yes, but her practical side said no.

With a sigh, she texted back.

Be down at your truck in five.

Then she took off her denim apron and went to change from her faded Mickey T-shirt into a light-weight cranberry cashmere sweater that was old, supersoft and comfy, but did nothing for her auburn hair and complexion.

No problem there. She certainly didn't care about making a great impression where Devlin was concerned. After dabbing away a dusting of flour on her chin, she locked the cabin door behind her and jogged down the hill.

Hiding away in her cabin only delayed the inevitable, right? Devlin was living at the ranch and so was she, an unfortunate coincidence that wasn't going to change anytime soon. She might as well do her best to be friendly and upbeat, no matter what he thought.

It didn't matter a bit.

Chloe smelled so good.

The moment she climbed into his truck, he could detect vanilla and chocolate, which made him long for her incredible cookies all over again.

He glanced at her a second time before putting the truck in gear, just in case she had a plate of something delicious in her hand and he'd missed it.

"What?" She flipped down the visor to look in the mirror, then flipped it back up and gave him a side-eye. "Is something wrong?"

"Just checking. I didn't want to miss seeing any cookies you might have over there."

"Sorry." She held up her empty hands, her dimples deepening as she smothered a grin. "I started working on my Grandma Lydia's chocolate cake today—though I kept making mistakes and didn't get very far. If and when I succeed, I'll try a sliver and give the rest to you. I… I try to watch my calories."

"I'll be happy to dispose of any extras, anytime." Turning onto the highway, he considered what he knew about her life after she and her dad had moved away from the ranch.

Very little, except that now he knew she liked to bake but didn't want to eat what she made. Which made little sense, but it certainly worked for him. "Just curious... Why do you bake when you don't want to eat any of it?"

She fidgeted in her seat and looked out at the Montana landscape. "Well, promise you won't laugh?"

"Why would I?"

"My mom did," she said glumly. "Moms are supposed to be positive and supportive, or so I've heard. Mine thinks I'm wasting my time. She thinks I should just concentrate on my new job, after what hap—"

She broke off sharply, which piqued his curiosity even more. After what? And how any of that could relate to making cookies and cakes, he had no idea. He shot a quick glance at her. "Now you have me in suspense."

She took a long time to answer, as if choosing her words carefully. "I could've gone straight from Minneapolis to my new job in Kansas City. But I figured I had enough savings to cover a few months of total concentration on something I *really* want—and need to get done—before being caught up in a boring nine-to-five job. And coming out here—to the ranch where I spent so much of my childhood—seemed like the perfect place. Sort of like a working vacation."

At her grim tone, he had so many questions that he didn't know where to begin, but she seemed so guarded that he suspected there were things she had no intention of sharing. "It's a little hard to imagine you taking a job you already dislike."

She sighed heavily. "It's even hard for me to imagine it, honestly. But after college I...um...really need the money to pay off my debts. My sister and brother-in-law want me to manage their income properties, and they offered me a salary I just can't refuse."

"What job would you love more? Does it involve cookies?" That earned him a wistful smile.

"That and a bit more."

But after driving three more miles en route to Pine Bend, she still hadn't elaborated.

"I did promise I wouldn't laugh," he reminded her.

"Okay," she said with a sigh. "I told you about my creative-writing major. I've always wanted to be a writer, but working full-time and finishing graduate school at night never left enough time. I did complete a young-adult novel that I worked on for my creative-writing thesis, and I've also completed my first draft of a cookbook. Now I figure a few months of total concentration will give me a good start on my revisions."

"Why would your mom laugh at that?"

"Yeah, well…do you remember her at all? She didn't stay at the ranch very long when we first moved here. She's a very practical woman. She hated my dad's transient lifestyle, moving from one ranch job to the next. So when she left us, she got herself an office job that she doesn't enjoy, but she's plowing through anyway, just to reach retirement. Can you imagine? Sixteen more years of a job she hates, while her life is ticking by. So to her, my writing is a foolish waste of time. She wants me to focus on a regular job and forget about anything else."

"And not be happy."

"Yeah, but that doesn't matter. Dad wasn't exactly a consistent provider, so life is all about security to her."

"I don't know anything about being a writer, but I'd expect most of them need regular jobs while chasing their dreams."

"That's what I tried to tell her. And that's what I'm planning to do. But at this point it isn't a topic she and I can even discuss. At twenty-nine, I'm old enough to make my own choices, don't you think?"

"Yes, you are." Devlin pulled into the vet clinic parking lot, turned off the ignition and rested a wrist on the top of the steering wheel. "I hope this goes well...and that you won't be disappointed."

She followed his gaze to the front of the clinic. "I want whatever is in the dog's best interest. I guess only the vet can tell us what that is."

He started to open his truck door and winced as a sharp pain arrowed down his neck.

"What's wrong?" She twisted in her seat to look at him, her eyes opened wide. "Are you all right?"

"Just a little sore. No big deal."

"You look like you're in a lot of pain. Did you get bucked off or something?"

Affronted, he shook his head. "That hasn't happened since I was six. I've started some weights and running."

"And target practice. I heard you again yesterday. How did it go?"

That was a topic he didn't plan to discuss. Not until he was far, far more accurate. He'd been a better shot with his BB gun in kindergarten.

He unbuckled his seat belt and glanced over at her. The red sweater she was wearing brought color to her cheeks and seemed to highlight the ruby tones in her hair, but it also brought back memories of much happier times...and sad ones. "That cashmere sweater looks good on you."

"How in the world do you know it's cashmere? What guy would even know that?"

He shrugged. "Good guess."

"No, really." She looked completely fascinated, now. "I'm impressed."

"My...my girlfriend wore cashmere whenever she didn't need to be in uniform. Gina always said it felt soft as a cloud."

"What a perfect description. I totally agree with her,

though cashmere wasn't in my budget until I started finding vintage sweaters on eBay." Chloe unbuckled her seat belt. "So, is she still in the military?"

"No."

She angled a bright smile in his direction. "Will she be coming to the ranch?"

She could not have asked a more painful question. He felt a shard of ice pierce his heart.

"She died." He opened his door and strode into the vet clinic, though he could feel her shocked gaze fixed on his back and knew the topic wasn't finished.

Why on earth had he said *that*? He instantly knew he'd made a grave tactical error when Chloe's eyes had opened even wider, and wished he could call his words back.

She'd always been like a determined beagle on the trail of a rabbit, and now he could see the days and weeks ahead, with Chloe peppering him with questions about Gina that he didn't want to answer.

Some things were too private, too raw to share. Especially about a tragedy that had been all his fault.

Chapter Six

His girlfriend. Of course he'd had a girlfriend. Probably a lot of them over the years. So why did the thought
feel like a volley of arrows hitting her square in the
heart?

For a drive that started so well, things had certainly
taken a turn for the worse on the way to town.

Given his obvious brush off last night and the way
he'd laughed at her after she'd left the barn, she'd figured they would have cool interactions at best from
now on. Yet he'd really been rather sweet to ask about
her baking, and he'd seemed sincerely interested in her
writing.

But the moment she'd innocently asked about his
girlfriend, his voice had turned cold as ice. He'd said
Gina *wore* cashmere whenever she could be out of uniform. Chloe had thought that meant she was simply out
of the military, out of his life or that it had been just a
slip of the tongue.

Whatever the circumstances of the poor woman's
death, Devlin had made it crystal clear that their relationship was not a topic for discussion, and it was none

of her business. Perhaps he was still grieving deeply for her and the topic was too wrenching to even discuss?

Chloe wouldn't ever bring it up again.

Bonnie led them into a back room with two walls of stainless steel kennels stacked four high, and larger pens across the back wall.

Amidst a cacophony of barking, Bonnie took them to the farthest corner, where a warming lamp hung over a pen. "Dr. Weldon had us clean her up last night before doing the surgery. We did our best, given her wounds, and we had to clip the worst of the matting, so she looks a bit threadbare. But before she goes home, we'll give her another bath. She'll look even better."

"What?" Devlin looked between Chloe and the vet tech.

Chloe raised her voice and repeated Bonnie's words as she reached the pen.

"Oh, my word," Chloe breathed as she looked down at the stray. She was lying on a thick foam bed, sleeping. "You've done an amazing job!"

The poor thing had been a bedraggled, matted grey mop before, almost indistinguishable as a dog. Now, though her matted hair had been clipped short in numerous places, her remaining coat was fluffy and nearly white, except for a solid black ear.

Chloe stepped around an IV bag hanging from a pole next to the pen, with a tube running to the dog's good front leg. The other front leg was encased in a bright green cast. Once again she spoke loudly over the barking dogs. "How long will she need the splint and bandages?"

"We'll have to see how well she does." Bonnie studied the IV, then smiled fondly at the sleeping dog. "She's on IV antibiotics and fluids right now, and is eating special, high-nutrition dog food. A dog of this size and breed should weigh at least thirty pounds more than she does. But her appetite is good, so she should do well. And she's a complete sweetheart. You can see she is so grateful for attention and a soft bed. Have you decided on a name?"

Bonnie had caught the hint and she spoke more loudly, though she was facing the dog instead of Devlin as she spoke.

Devlin's gaze skated over to Chloe, and she saw pure frustration in his eyes. "Bonnie, could we step out of the kennel? It's too hard for Dev and me to hear in here."

They followed the tech out into the hall, where she closed the door behind them to mute the barking. "I know," she said with a smile. "All of those dogs are wanting to go home. I was just trying to ask about what name you want to give her."

Chloe saw Devlin watching the woman's lips as she spoke.

He shrugged. "No idea. Chloe?"

"She looks like a polar bear to me—or she will, once all of her fur grows back. Bear? Or Tramp, since she's been wandering for so long? I like Daisy. Or—"

"Whoa." Devlin held up a hand. "This could be just temporary if someone comes to claim her. What do you think, Bonnie?"

She smiled, the corners of her eyes crinkling. "I don't think we have a Daisy as a patient these days. I think it's a good fit for a gentle pooch like her."

Chloe nodded. "And sweet for an older dog. At least I'd guess she's not very young. Does Dr. Weldon have any idea how old she is?"

"It's harder to tell in adult dogs. You can't detect muzzle whitening given her color, but the vet guessed four to six, maybe seven years, as her eyes are still clear and bright, and she doesn't show signs of arthritic pain. But it's just a guess."

"Then Daisy it is, and she's one lucky dog." Devlin gave Chloe a lopsided grin. "Because if the twins had anything to do with naming her, I'll bet she would be Fluffy."

"Dr. Weldon thought this was Leonard Farley's service dog." Chloe bit her lower lip, not wanting to bring the subject up yet, knowing it was the right thing to do. "Still, there's surely a chance she was abandoned or even lost. What do you recommend we do?"

"Given her condition and breed, it would be a mighty big coincidence if Daisy belonged to anyone else. We just don't see many Great Pyrenees around here," Bonnie said firmly. "If she was his service dog, she probably stayed with his body for a long time after Leonard died, then maybe got desperate for food and finally left. Or maybe she just panicked and ran. We've seen it before. Say there's a car crash or a house fire—the dog escapes and then just runs and runs until hopelessly lost. Sometimes they're found. Sometimes not."

"But if Daisy does have a family, children missing her…"

"Well, dear, you're certainly welcome to put up a notice on our billboard. Do you not want to keep her?"

"Of course I do, if I know there isn't a heartbroken owner somewhere." She gave Devlin an uncertain glance. "Though maybe Devlin should have her since he insists on covering the vet bills."

Devlin lifted his hands, palms forward. "Nope. I'll only be around for a short while, and I have no idea where I'll end up or what kind of place I'll have next. She wouldn't have a good home with me."

Bonnie smiled at Chloe kindly. "Then I'm 99 percent sure you've got yourself a dog. But if you insist on advertising, there are also billboards at the Laundromat and the grocery store. Just be vague about your description and sure you don't put a photo on your flyers. Using 'big white dog' would suffice."

"Because…"

"Someone might think they could nab a Great Pyrenees for free. But if they have to describe their lost dog to you, probably only the real owner—or a friend of Leonard's—would know about that totally black ear. I could be wrong, but far as I know that's an unusual color for that breed."

"Good idea."

"You might even want to ask for proof—like a family photo with the dog or something." Bonnie lifted a shoulder. "Just to be sure. I know you wouldn't want her to fall into the wrong hands."

After picking up calf-milk replacer and a half dozen red-mineral and white-salt blocks at the feed store, Devlin turned the truck for home.

Chloe watched him from the corner of her eye, feeling pensive and unsure of whether she should say anything or not. He'd been less distant today. Would this be a good time to ask something personal? What were old friends for but complete honesty?

"So, Devlin," she said in her normal tone. "Pretty good news about Daisy, right?"

His brow furrowed. He cut a quick glance at her before turning his attention back to the arrow-straight road leading to the foothills.

She raised her voice. *"Devlin."*

That small, telltale muscle jerked along the side of his jaw. "What?"

"I hope you won't mind me asking, but it seems like you have trouble hearing sometimes," she said tactfully. "Did that happen while you were in the military?"

His mouth flattened to a straight, hard line and his eyes narrowed.

"I'm only asking because I'm concerned. It's got to be tough, missing out on what people are saying."

"I hear you just fine," he bit out, his attention riveted on the highway.

"That's because I've learned I have to stand closer and talk a lot louder. And I make sure I'm facing you, since I noticed that you read lips."

He shot a look of disbelief and irritation at her.

"Honest, I'd just like to help."

He heaved a sigh, his grip on the steering wheel turning his knuckles white. "And how can you do what no one else could?"

The sharp edge in his voice made her feel like he'd sliced off a corner of her heart, but she couldn't stop now. "Did you get second opinions? Research procedures and success rates across the country for fixing whatever is wrong? Or did you just give up when a busy intern said nothing could be done?"

He didn't answer.

"I'm only asking because I care, Dev. Did they try—really try—to find a hearing aid that would work?"

"*None* have worked well. I'm wearing some right now, though they're almost invisible. They make little difference."

His voice was low and level, and brimming with such frustration that she didn't know what to say.

He drove several miles in silence, his jaw clenched

and his attention riveted on the road ahead. "Look, I appreciate your concern, but the docs were clear about what I can expect," he said finally, slanting an impatient glance in her direction. "I have trouble with sound in the mid-to-higher range, and given my injuries, it won't get better."

"But still, with advances in—"

"No. I'll probably keep partial hearing on the left, but they think I might eventually lose my hearing entirely on the right. I also lost partial vision in my right eye. With that and my shoulder, a single bomb blast ended my active-duty career in the Marines. None of that is going to change."

"I'm so sorry." Her eyes burning, she bowed her head, knowing she could never hope to fully understand the emotional and physical trauma he had been through. She tried to dredge up an encouraging smile. "Then again, you are truly blessed. It could have been worse, right?"

"You think I don't know that? That I don't think every single day about the friends I lost? The ones who are now severely disabled?" He gave her an incredulous look. "Wonderful guys. Husbands, fathers. Guys who would've made a bigger impact on this world than me. I *know* I have no right to complain, and I try not to. I was just explaining since you seem so all-fired curious. And now that topic is closed."

If only she could eat her words.

She'd only wanted to be his cheerleader and to bring up the positives in his life. Instead she'd inadvertently been condescending and disrespectful, and if he never forgave her presumptuous words, she wouldn't be surprised. It did not pay to be an oblivious Pollyanna.

When he pulled to a stop by the barn to unload the

back of the pickup, she gathered her courage. "I'm sorry, Dev. I truly meant no disrespect and I won't bring it up again. I just want to offer you one thing. If it would be any help, I could start teaching you to sign while I'm here. Then you'd at least have a start at it if…the doctors are right about you becoming deaf later on."

But just as she expected, he didn't answer.

After unloading the pickup, Devlin saddled one of the two-year-olds and got to work in the arena.

Yesterday the young mare had been calm and steady. Today she shied at the motion of a barn cat just outside the arena. Threw in a spine-jarring crow hop when he eased her into a lope. Fought the bit when he asked her to back up.

And then he finally realized that it was him, not her.

He took a slow breath and forced himself to let go of the tension in his spine and the emotions tying his stomach into one big knot. He tried to set aside Chloe's words. *Sign language.* A crutch he didn't want to even think about.

He rode the mare around the arena at an easy walk before pivoting and trying the lope in a different direction. This time she made the transition smoothly.

Deciding to stop on a good note, he dismounted in the center of the arena and took her back to the barn. Then he worked the rest of the horses one after another until it was time for chores.

It wasn't until he swung out of the saddle on the last horse that he noticed Chloe watching him through the picture window in the tack room, an elbow propped on the window sill, her chin resting on her upraised palm. He felt his heart take an extra beat at just the sight of her.

But her expression was pensive, not friendly. She didn't respond when he nodded to her. And she was gone by the time he led the mare into the barn. Had she been there the whole time?

The bigger question was why she'd even bothered.

He'd been mulling over their trip to town, replaying all of the ways their conversation had gone terribly wrong. The awkward, tension-filled exchange over things he refused to talk about with anyone. Her chipper effort to be positive—even while zeroing in on the most painful parts of his life like a heat-seeking missile with perfect aim, ripping away the scabs from the places he'd tried his hardest to forget.

As if she could help.

She always *meant* well. He probably owed her an apology. But there was nothing she could do. Every effort at the VA to save his hearing and improve the eyesight in his right eye had resulted in failure and bitter disappointment, until he finally accepted the truth and decided to give up and move on.

Until he'd learned about the job in New York and the chance to start a new and exciting career, anyway.

Now that he could see a bright future ahead, he would do everything in his power to avoid throwing that chance away—if it meant running and lifting weights until he dropped, followed by every physical-therapy exercise in the world.

But Chloe's assumption about finding a miraculous cure to improve his hearing was just flat wrong.

After letting the twins' pup go outside for a while, he threw the ball and played fetch, though *assault* was probably the operative term.

With each retrieve, forty pounds of half-grown puppy hurtled into his knees, nearly knocking him flat, or launched joyously at his chin, almost decking him twice. It was like having a buffalo running amok.

The pup would go on all day, nonstop, but twenty minutes was more than enough for Devlin.

His cell phone chirped as he was heading for the laundry room to fill Poofy's food and water bowls. When he saw his brother's name on the screen, he switched the phone to speaker—on the loudest volume—and put it on the counter so he could feed the pup and grab a cup of coffee. "So, how's it going? Good vacation, or is it time to come home?"

"The girls loved the two days at Disneyland. Now we're at a hotel outside San Diego, waiting to meet up with Lindsey and her stepmom at a restaurant. I hope this goes well."

Knowing his youngest cousin, Devlin had his doubts. After Lindsey had dropped the twins off at the ranch the Christmas before last, she'd completely disappeared for a year to lead a wild life. Still, according to Jess, she was finally doing better, had reconnected with her estranged stepmother, and had been in and out of residential treatment facilities for her drug addictions and depression.

Poofy pawed at Devlin's leg and he bent down to stroke his silky fur. "Are they excited about seeing their mom again?"

"Subdued, actually. Since our adoption papers were finalized, they've rarely spoken about her. We have her photo on the mantle and are ready and willing to talk about her anytime, but they just aren't interested."

"Maybe they're afraid you're going to give them back." Though no one had said as much, Devlin could guess at the kind of uncertain, vagabond life the twins had experienced before being taken in by Jess and Grandma Betty.

"Lindsey insisted on fully relinquishing her rights to us, and for that I'm thankful. When I told her we wanted to come for a short visit this week, her first response was 'okay, but I don't want the girls back, if that's what you're thinking.'" Jess sighed heavily. "I'm just glad she has a clear head about not being capable of parenting the girls. She's led a very troubled life."

"It was a done deal anyway, once her rights were terminated. Right?"

"Right. I just hope I'm doing the right thing by maintaining some contact between her and the girls. The social workers have encouraged it, but I guess we'll see how this little visit goes. So, how is everything back home?"

"I'm working the two-year-olds, and they're fine. Ten more calves born and two new foals—nice paint fillies—since you left. I'll text you some photos."

"Good news." There was a hint of a grin in his voice. "Anything else?"

At that moment Devlin knew Jess had known all along about Chloe's 'surprise' arrival.

"You could've told me."

"What?"

"Before y'all left, Betty mentioned that someone would be coming to rent a cabin, but she didn't say who."

"Ahhh." Jess cleared his throat. "So how's *that* going?"

"What do you think? It's *Chloe*. Surely you remember her?"

"I remember a sweet little girl who followed you everywhere. By now she's surely a pretty gal who has plenty of handsome, successful guys chasing after her." The laughter in Jess's voice was unmistakable. "She probably wouldn't give a cowboy like you the time of day, little brother."

"Thanks," Devlin retorted. "But being left alone would be my dream. It isn't quite working out that way."

This time Jess laughed out loud. "You've got just five days 'til we're home, and with your tact and charm, I'm sure you'll survive that long. Tell her we're all looking forward to seeing her again, will you?"

Devlin heard Jess talking to someone in the background, then he came back to his phone. "Gotta go. Lindsey and her stepmom just pulled into the parking lot."

The connection went dead.

Devlin looked into the pup's dark, soulful eyes. "Five days left, buddy. Seems like a long, long time to me. How are we going to manage?"

Though with the way Chloe was steering clear of him, maybe it wouldn't be so hard after all.

Chapter Seven

On Saturday morning Chloe drove to town without bothering to mention her plans to Devlin. There was no reason she needed to, of course, and she preferred to go alone. The thought of another awkward conversation during the interminable length of open highway between the ranch and town made her mind up for sure.

After stopping at the vet clinic on the west edge of town to check on Daisy's progress and drop off a Lost Dog flyer, she thumbtacked another flyer on the bulletin board in the Laundromat and then headed for Millers, the only grocery store in town, to do the same.

She'd stopped there briefly to buy perishables when passing through Pine Bend on her way to the ranch, but she'd been in a rush after driving seven hundred miles in one day, and hadn't taken a good look around.

There wasn't much to see.

No bigger than a three-stall garage, it had the basics but not much selection, and the prices were steep. The teenage girl at the single checkout lane idly glanced at her as she walked in, then continued staring at her cell phone.

The only other customer was a slender woman in

tight black jeans and an even tighter black sweater, with a bouffant platinum-blond hairdo, who brought her cart close by.

She gave Chloe a curious look, then smiled. "Pardon me, ma'am. But your name wouldn't be Chloe, would it?"

Startled, Chloe searched her face, trying to remember who she might be. A childhood friend from the elementary school in town, maybe? "Yes. But I'm afraid I don't remember your name. I haven't been here for many years."

"I don't expect we've ever met. I'm pretty new in town myself, and I remember how hard it was for me at first, when I didn't know a soul. So I always try to say hello."

Still mystified, Chloe smiled back at her. "Why, thank you."

The woman leaned closer, as if ready to tell a secret. "Betty Foster told me you were coming to stay at Langford Ranch. She told me to watch for a pretty stranger in town with reddish hair, so I took a wild guess. I'm Darla Peterson, Abby's new stepmom." She winked. "Though I'm not much older than she is."

"She's the twins' nanny, right?"

"Yes, ma'am, and Jess's new fiancée. You've got it. Are you getting along okay out at the ranch with most everyone gone?" She locked on to Chloe's gaze as if trying to make sure all was well. "I hear Devlin Langford isn't very sociable, so if there's anything I can do for you, or you want to stop by for coffee sometime, just let me know."

Chloe liked this chipper woman already. "That's very kind of you."

Darla pulled a pen and a crumpled receipt from her

purse, scribbled down a number, and handed it to Chloe.
"This is my cell number, just in case you need it. I'm
sure we'll see each other again soon, though. Don and I
go over to the Langford ranch for Sunday dinner sometimes, and for holidays. How long will you be here?"

"Three months at the most."

"Wonderful! We'll see each other at Easter dinner, then. It will be so nice to have a new friend." She
glanced at her watch and her eyes widened. "Oh, my
goodness—I've got to run. Don's out in the truck and he
must think I've fallen off the planet. Nice meeting you!"

Chloe watched her bustle away to the checkout line
and smiled. With Betty and now this livewire in her
life, Abby was certainly blessed. But even more so, because she and Jess had found each other. He'd always
been the steady, hardworking and dependable Langford brother—and would surely be a wonderful husband, too.

After buying her groceries, Chloe drove farther east
on Main Street to see what had changed since she'd
lived here, expecting mostly the empty storefronts of a
dusty, dying town.

Millie's Coffee Shop was new, along with a number
of touristy businesses geared toward the folks passing through Pine Bend on their way to the mountains.
High-country adventure outfitters. A bike shop with
pricey mountain bikes in the front window. A florist
and several gift shops. A sportswear shop displaying
running gear.

Over the treetops to the south, the white, old-fashioned
steeple of the community church still peeked about the
rooftops and pines, bringing back a landslide of memories she hadn't thought of in years.

Her dad had never attended except for Christmas and

Easter, and Gus Langford had been determined never to set foot in the church again after Heather's funeral. For as long as Chloe had lived at the ranch, he had kept that promise, except for his wife's funeral less than a year later, and finally, she supposed, his own. Whatever his other faults had been, when he gave his word, it was cast in iron.

But sweet Grandma Betty, bless her heart, had herded the boys to church every Sunday, and she'd always brought Chloe along too, with a promise of thickly frosted donuts and chocolate milk at the tiny café on Main if they were all quiet and paid attention.

She drove on slowly and glanced at the few pedestrians on the sidewalk, who all looked unfamiliar. Would she still recognize anyone in town? Probably not. She'd been just eleven when she and Dad had moved away, and the locals surely wouldn't remember her, either.

Even if a few folks recalled a ranch foreman's skinny little girl with red hair and freckles, they might not recognize her now that her hair had gradually darkened to deep auburn.

At the end of the four-block strip of businesses on the main road through town, there were a couple of vacant lots, then a gas station offering mechanic services, though a hand-lettered sign in the front picture window said Closed for Funeral—Credit Cards Still Okay on Gas Pumps.

Despite all of the years she'd been away, and the changes in what was now a burgeoning little town, she felt strangely at home here, she thought with an inward smile. It was actually going to be hard to leave once her three months were up.

After filling up her gas tank, she turned around and

headed back to the ranch, humming along to a song on a country radio station turned up high.

The SUV suddenly jerked and seemed to sink on one side.

She groaned when she heard the flappity-flappity sound of a blown tire. Of all places—midway between the ranch and town, with vast open country as far as she could see and not a ranch in sight. Her auto-club towing service—did they even answer calls in middle-of-nowhere Montana?—had lapsed months ago, and she already knew the gas station in town was closed.

After pulling as far over as she could onto the gravel shoulder of the highway, she went to check. Sure enough, the back left tire wasn't only flat, it was blown beyond repair. And when she went to retrieve her spare, it was missing.

She sighed heavily. Just before leaving Minneapolis, she'd had an oil change and had asked the guys to check all of the fluids, the tires and even the spare. Had they taken it out and forgotten to put it back?

Sliding back into the driver's seat, she reached for her cell phone. *No service.*

She tipped her head back on the headrest. It would be more than a seven-mile hike in either direction, through desolate country, and the thought of leaving the protection of her vehicle made her shudder.

Maybe the majority of the drivers passing by were good people, but what about the rest, who might see a lone, young woman as easy prey?

She eyed the rise of the road a good quarter mile ahead. Maybe there'd be better reception up there. If she crept slowly along the shoulder, the tire would be ruined and probably the wheel rim, as well. But could driving that distance cause even more serious damage? Hopefully not.

Praying she was right, she stayed on the shoulder of the road and eased the vehicle slowly up the next slope, then pulled even farther off the road and checked her phone. Two bars of reception out of five. *Yes!*

Heaving a sigh of relief, she called Devlin's number. The call went straight to voice mail. After leaving a message, she also sent a text.

Then she waited and waited as cars and semis whizzed by so fast that her SUV shook in the blasts of wind they each created.

With her lightly tinted windows, they likely couldn't see her while speeding by, yet stepping outside presented the possibility of even greater problems. She hadn't lived in a city and regularly watched the evening news for nothing.

A half hour later, Devlin still hadn't responded. Then an hour. For all she knew, he might not even be at the ranch, or maybe he'd left his phone in his cabin again and wouldn't check it until evening.

If yet another half hour passed, she would call her new best friend, Darla…though out here in ranch country, the woman could live an hour on the other side of Pine Bend. And how could Chloe impose on her then?

An old, dented Chevy pickup slowed as it went past, then executed a laborious U-turn and pulled up close to her back bumper.

Please Lord, a sweet old ranch lady would be perfect.

But when two hulking occupants stepped out of that rattletrap truck, she took one look and her heart lodged in her throat. She hit the locks. Turned the key in the ignition. Sent Devlin another text.

And when the two men leaned down to leer at her through the side windows of the SUV, she knew this was far worse than she'd even imagined.

Shifting the SUV into Drive, she hit the 911 speed-dial button on her phone, stomped on the accelerator and started to pray.

I'm scared. Please come.

Devlin hit sixty on the gravel lane out to the highway, then turned toward Pine Bend and floored the accelerator.

Her first text had arrived almost two hours ago, saying she'd blown a tire halfway home from town, but he'd left his cell phone in the tack room when he had gone to the meadow for target practice, followed by an hour-long run up into the foothills. He hadn't realized that she'd called.

The second message sounded much, much worse, and knowing Chloe, it wasn't just a complaint about waiting for him to show up.

He still hadn't seen any sign of her at five miles from the ranch, then six…

A half mile later he rounded a curve.

And there it was—praise the Lord.

Her SUV had gone off the road, down an embankment, broken through a barbwire fence to end up nose down in a shallow, dry creek bed. An old pickup was parked on the highway shoulder just above it, as if someone had stopped to help her.

But when Devlin pulled to a stop and jumped out of his vehicle, he instantly knew there'd been no *helping* involved.

His heart jerked in his chest.

One guy was slowly stalking Chloe way out into the sagebrush, as if he was a predator toying with prey.

His Chloe—in *danger*. That such a lowlife dared even to contemplate laying a hand on her sent adrenaline surging through Devlin.

His buddy—heavily muscled, with tattoo sleeves emblazoned up both arms—was moaning and bent nearly double by the side of her SUV, his hands at his tear-streaked face.

Clearly she must have pepper sprayed him at close range. *Good girl.* Still, it didn't pay to risk having him recover and then have to deal with them both.

Devlin reached him in a split second. "Hey, you—looking for trouble?"

"I guess you are," the man growled as he straightened, blearily glared at him and threw a hard left that just missed.

Cold fury surged through him as Devlin dropped him with a swift upper cut, then spun around, searched the back of the pickup and found some lengths of baling twine to tie the man's hands behind his back. He grabbed the keys out of the ignition.

The man's heavily muscled Neanderthal buddy had apparently kept enough distance from the pepper spray, and he was closing in on Chloe as she limped across the sagebrush-infested flatland. She wouldn't have a chance if he caught her.

Instinct born of his years in the Marines kicked in as Devlin took off down the slope, vaulted over the fence and raced toward them, his light footsteps muffled by the sandy ground beneath his feet and nearly silent.

Chloe began to curve back toward the highway. The man blocked off her path like a cutting horse singling out a steer, driving her farther from the view of any drivers passing by.

He abruptly stopped and started to turn, the blade of a knife glittering in one hand.

But Devlin was already on him, slamming him to the ground and twisting one hand high behind his back until he howled in pain. His knife slithered away across the ground.

Despite the man's stench of booze, sweat and cigarettes, Devlin leaned close. "I would be so happy if you chose to resist," he whispered harshly, "given what you were planning to do to that poor girl."

The man writhed beneath him. Devlin braced one knee against his spine and leaned heavily on it. "Go ahead, be difficult. But know that I could snap your neck with one hand. Easily."

"He's a Marine. I wouldn't test him if I were you." Chloe called out as she edged closer, still staying a safe distance away, her face ghostly white and her arms wrapped around her middle.

Devlin looked up at her, then did a double-take at a bruise already forming by her eye. "Did he *hit* you?"

"No—I just bumped my head when I started running, tripped and fell. No big deal."

Devlin searched her face. "Are you dizzy? Could you have been knocked out for a while?"

"No—or I never would've gotten away."

He wanted nothing more than to pull her into his arms for a long, comforting embrace, but the man beneath his knee started struggling harder and Devlin readjusted his grip. "After we're done here, you should go to the ER in Pine Bend."

"No. I'm fine. It would be a waste of time."

No matter what she thought, he would keep an eye

on her for a while. "You wouldn't happen to be wearing that leather belt again, would you?"

"First the pony, now this. I'd better never leave home without it," she said with a shaky laugh as she unfolded her arms, took off the belt and handed it over, then stepped well away.

She watched as Devlin jerked the man's other arm behind his back and twisted the narrow belt into a tight set of makeshift handcuffs, then hauled him roughly to his feet. "Wow. You're good at that."

"Just practice." Devlin surveyed her from head to toe. "Are you sure you're all right?"

She shuddered. "A whole lot better now. I owe you my life."

He picked up the knife with the edge of his shirt, careful not to leave his own fingerprints, and propelled the man forward with his other hand. He saw her wince as she took a step. "How bad is that ankle?"

"Just a little sprain, if that."

He offered her the crook of his elbow and slowed his pace when she took his arm.

She glanced up toward the highway. "Looks like a deputy has finally arrived."

"You got nothin' on me," the man snarled, shooting a glare towards Chloe. "I didn't even touch you. I'll be free in no time."

"Something tells me this isn't your first rodeo, buddy," Devlin said. "I'm a witness, this young lady will have plenty to say and you *will* be facing charges."

They met up with the deputy at Chloe's car. He already had the other man in handcuffs and shook his head as he pulled another set from the back of his belt. "Duane and Keith Dooley, together again. You know what the judge said the last time you boys got paroled, yet here you are. When will you ever learn?"

The deputy's deep, gravelly voice was easy for him to hear, and it brought back a landslide of memories. Devlin took a good look at the deputy and laughed. "Lance? It's been a long time."

Chloe glanced back and forth between them, her eyes narrowing on the deputy's name badge. "Lance Harrison? You two were buddies in high school."

"Yes, ma'am." Lifting a clipboard he'd left on the hood of her SUV, Lance took a pen from his front pocket. "I'm sure I can take a wild guess, but can you tell me exactly what happened here?"

Chloe visibly shivered. "I had a blown tire and I was waiting for help. These two guys saw me, did a U-turn on the highway and came after me. I tried driving on just the wheel rim, but didn't get far—they rammed my back bumper, I lost control and ended up in the ditch."

Lance nodded. "And then?"

"I had pepper spray in my glovebox." She bit her lower lip. "I disabled one of them, but then the other guy—"

"Duane."

"Yeah, Duane hit the cannister out of my hand and grabbed me. I got him in the stomach with my elbow and took off. But then he came after me, threatening me with his knife. He kept taunting me, like he really enjoyed the chase."

The deputy took a long look at her face. "I see some bruising. Did one of them hit you?"

"No, I fell while trying to get away."

He wrote something else on his clipboard. "I've actually been looking for these two, for parole violations. They'll be finishing their full sentences, and with this incident, that should put them away for a long time." Lance finished writing his notes. "I noticed that you have Minnesota plates. Will you be in the area for a while?"

"Three months over at the Langford ranch. I'm renting a cabin there."

"Good. I might need to talk to you again later. Want me to call for a wrecker?"

Devlin hunkered down next to the blown tire and battered rim. "I'll take care of it for her. If I don't have the right size wheel back home, I'll pick one up in town on Monday. Thanks, though."

The deputy pulled a business card from his pocket and flipped it over to Devlin. "Give me a call sometime. We should get together and knock back a few drinks at Red's for old-time's sake, eh?"

The place had been a dive with a bad reputation in the old days, where underage drinkers slipped in the back door and were welcomed with a wink of the eye and a big ole Montana howdy. It was probably even worse now and not a place Dev wanted to be.

He felt Chloe's gaze burning into the back of his head. "Let's meet for dinner instead. Give me a call when you're free."

He helped march the two men over to the patrol car and load them into the back seat, then he went back to Chloe's SUV and waited while she retrieved her phone, purse and jacket.

"I've also got groceries in the back," she said, lifting the tailgate.

The tension of the last twenty minutes slipped away as he looked down at her, his heart thudding. Bone-deep relief filled his chest over what might have been if he hadn't seen her text message. If he'd been too far away. Or if he hadn't taken her seriously.

Without conscious thought, he pulled her into an embrace, then lowered his mouth to hers for a sweet kiss. But he still couldn't let her go. *Thank you, Lord.*

She was *safe*. Warm and breathing and beautiful, his sweet Chloe, but even now she could have been left out amongst the sagebrush, where her body might never have been found.

She melted against him, and he lost track of how long he held her until she finally stepped back and wrapped her arms around her middle. "I don't even know what to say, Dev," she whispered. "Except thanks. From the bottom of my heart."

He took her things up to his vehicle, then returned and offered her the crook of his elbow once again, to help her back up to the highway.

But she seemed unsteady on her feet, and when she stumbled, he scooped her up in one swift motion and carried her up the slope. She felt as light as a kitten, and though he felt a deep ache in his right shoulder, her soft warmth made him want to hold on tightly and never let go.

"Wait…" she protested, her cheeks turning scarlet. "I can walk just fine."

"It would take twice as long, and if you slip on this gravel, you could get hurt even worse." He put her down by the passenger side of his SUV and opened the door. "Here you go. Consider it part of the Langford Rescue Service."

She managed a weak laugh at that. "For which I am extremely grateful. You will never know how much."

"I'm sure I can guess," he said dryly.

When they were both belted in and heading back to

the ranch, she tipped her head slightly and gave him a curious look. "Would you *really* have broken Duane's neck if he kept resisting?"

Devlin snorted. "Of course not. But he didn't know that. Intimidation can sometimes save a lot of effort."

He glanced over at her. She was shaking now; probably because her adrenaline was fading and the reality of the danger she'd faced was settling in. "I would've been here faster, but I spent the morning working the horses and my phone was in the tack room. Sorry. I left the minute I saw your messages."

"Believe me, I'm not complaining." She settled against the back of her seat, her eyes closed. "It's my fault. I figured I didn't need to tell you I was leaving for town. It's not like we're…um…like we have a personal connection or anything. But I should have said something. You might've wondered why I wasn't back yet and checked your phone sooner. Maybe none of this would have happened."

"Hindsight is always better," he said, glancing in his rearview mirror before passing a slow-moving tractor on the highway. "Don't dwell on it. It never changes a thing."

He nearly laughed at his own words. It certainly didn't—and he'd had almost a year to prove just how true that was.

Chapter Eight

She knew Devlin had been a Marine, in a dangerous career spent largely in the Middle East. But until today she hadn't truly realized the full extent of what he was.

A warrior.

A true hero.

A man who had just saved her life.

And a man whose warm embrace had made her feel loved and safe and whole again after one of the most terrifying moments of her life.

How did she reconcile all of that with her memories of the teenager he'd been—the wild boy who got into fights at school and got drunk with his equally wild buddies on too many occasions to count?

Lance Harrison had been one of the worst, and now the two of them were going to get together again. Were they finally mature, responsible adults who had put those youthful indiscretions behind them, or were they like her dad, for whom the seductive lure of the next drink meant more than a school conference, a birthday party, a father-daughter dance?

Since she'd arrived, she hadn't seen so much as an

empty beer can or liquor bottle anywhere on the ranch. So was Devlin beyond all of that now?

Not my business, she thought as she took another wrap of elastic bandage around her ankle, then carefully stood next to her sofa to test the result. Wincing, she tried taking a step, then another. Good enough. The Tylenol she'd taken for her headache ought to help her ankle, too.

She would be forever grateful for the way Dev had rescued her today. But she would never dare act on the rush of tangled emotions she'd felt when he lifted her so easily—despite his damaged shoulder—and carried her up to his SUV like some superhero.

Held against the warmth of his broad chest, with his heart thudding against her side, she felt her own heart start to race and her nerves tingle. It was the kind of moment she'd dreamed of as a little girl with stars in her eyes. And his kiss…even now the thought of it made her shiver.

But she had only to remember her latest romantic disaster in Minneapolis to reaffirm how blind she was when it came to judging character. *Gullible* and *naïve* could be her middle names. And thanks to Thad, she'd been reminded that unconditional trust was something to fear.

She limped to the kitchen and checked the temperature setting on the slow cooker, inhaling the rich aroma of her grandmother's *boeuf bourguignon*, a rich beef stew redolent with pearl onions, bacon, burgundy, garlic and a bouquet garni—flavorful herbs held in a little cheesecloth bag to infuse even more aromatic flavor.

"Grandma, you were amazing," she murmured to herself as she pulled a brown-sugar pound cake out of the oven, tested it with a toothpick and set it on the cooling rack. She'd just slipped a batch of cheddar-cheese biscuits into the oven when she heard a knock on the door.

A little shiver of anticipation—or was it fear?—snaked down her spine.

But she was safe here. This was surely just Devlin arriving on time for supper, and nothing to worry about.

Yet she found herself wishing that Daisy was already here, ready to bark at the approach of anyone nearing her cabin. At least then she would never be caught by surprise.

"It's just me," Devlin called out.

It was silly to feel such a rush of relief. Honestly, who else would be out on this remote ranch—much less on a narrow path leading to three small, privately owned cabins?

Yet just hours earlier, this day had brought danger, and it was hard to file away that sense of jeopardy and fear just because the Dooleys had been arrested and shoved into a patrol car. "Screen door's unlocked. Come on in."

He walked in, his Stetson in one hand, and took a deep breath. "Something smells amazing."

"More of my grandma's recipes, but with some tweaks here and there." She tipped her head toward the slow cooker. "Grandma made her *boeuf bourguignon* in the oven, but the slow cooker seemed like an easier way to go, so I'm testing it out. I'm just glad I started it this morning, before…" She swallowed hard and suppressed the waver in her voice. "Before going to town."

He gave her a long, searching look. "It was quite a day. How are you doing?"

Usually people who asked that question really didn't want to know, but with his gaze riveted on hers and that intense expression, she knew he wasn't just making small talk.

Still, she was only a little woozy after her fall, and her headache seemed to be subsiding. She might've hit her head a bit harder than she'd thought, but Devlin didn't need to know that. He'd probably make her go to the ER for a checkup that wasn't necessary at all.

And one she definitely couldn't afford.

"Pretty good. Everything that happened keeps running through my thoughts—like a movie that keeps restarting, over and over."

"That's no surprise. Would you feel safer in the main house? No one is there except the girls' puppy, and he stays in his kennel at night. I'm sure Abby wouldn't mind if you used her room."

She spared that option just a brief thought. Alone in that huge, rambling house with all of those darkened rooms? This snug little cabin felt more secure. "Thanks, but I'm fine right here."

"You could bring the puppy up here to stay with you, if you want company."

"That's tempting, but no. He's probably better off where he is."

"My thought exactly. Jess said he's still destructive, and if he isn't closed in his fenced yard, he has to be watched every second, or he'll either destroy something or run off. Apparently having a complete pair of shoes is pretty rare around here."

She smiled. "Sounds like fun."

The oven timer dinged, and she turned away to pull the pan of biscuits from the oven and slather the tops with melted garlic butter. Then she grabbed a wide baking dish of still-warm, lightly steamed fresh asparagus from the counter, sprinkled on some grated parmesan and slid it into the oven on Broil.

Devlin cleared his throat. "I talked to Lance on my way up here. Just so you know, the Dooleys' probation officer has been informed of their capture, and she has contacted a judge about revoking their probation. They're already being transferred to the county correctional center. With the additional charges they'll be facing from today, they won't be free for years."

"Good. I'm glad to hear it." She looked down at the fragrant golden biscuits. The news was a relief, to be sure. Yet even standing in this cabin, with a protector like Devlin just feet away, she still felt fear and vulnerability roiling through her midsection.

Today had been a random, unexpected situation. Maybe this incident was over, but how easily could something else like that happen again?

Shaking off her thoughts, she rescued the asparagus dish from the broiler and settled it on a trivet, pasted a smile on her face and turned around. "I think everything is ready. *Boeuf bourgnignon* in the big slow cooker, sour cream mashed potatoes in the smaller one. Parmesan asparagus, cheddar biscuits and then there's a dessert. I guess I forgot about making a salad."

His awed expression was that of a man who hadn't eaten in months. "This…this all looks perfect and smells amazing. How on earth did you manage to do so much?"

"I've always liked to cook, I guess—and it helps me relax." She lifted a shoulder in a faint shrug. "I sure needed it today. And I wanted you to come for a dinner as a way to thank you, but please—give me lots of honest feedback. You'll be helping me if you do."

* * *

He'd had decent food in the military, and certainly there'd been plenty of it. He'd had great restaurant dinners with Gina when they were both stateside.

But he couldn't remember a single meal that looked as appetizing and memorable as this one, though it wasn't just the incredible menu.

There could have been no dinner at all.

No Chloe to bustle around in the kitchen.

He couldn't stop thinking about how close she'd come to an assault. Maybe even death.

Out in that isolated landscape of gritty, arid soil and sagebrush, no one passing on the highway would've seen Duane's attack. And what were the chances that the Dooleys would have left her alive to call the sheriff and testify against them?

Zero.

If he hadn't checked his phone when he did, she would already be dead.

"Is something wrong? You'll tell me, right? Too much seasoning—or not enough?"

He looked down, realized he'd barely touched his food, and met her worried eyes. "It's all wonderful."

"Yeah, right." she said, her gaze skating across his plate. "I can tell you're savoring every bite. So, what's the problem?"

You, he thought, an unfamiliar ache settling deep in his chest.

He'd spent twelve years in the military, and he'd seen more than his fair share of battle. He'd expected it and had learned to steel his emotions as much as any man could.

But this was *his* Chloe. The earnest little girl with red pigtails and a gap-toothed smile who had been his shadow. Even now the thought of the Dooleys daring to touch her filled him with rage.

He set his fork aside. "I just can't do this meal justice. I keep thinking about what could have happened if I hadn't reached you in time."

"Everything turned out fine. End of story," she said so softly that he had to read her lips. "You arrived like a superhero and saved me in the nick of time."

A river of ice cascaded through him.

He didn't answer. He couldn't. *A hero?* Hardly. He had only to think of the people he'd failed and the price they'd paid, to clarify just how much of a hero he was. He inevitably lost those whom he loved the most.

His little sister. His mother. Gina. Everyone he'd ever loved, really.

Chloe tipped her head and seemed to look into his eyes to read his deepest thoughts. She sighed, her shoulders slumping as she leaned forward to rest her hand on his. "You still feel responsible for Heather's accident," she said flatly. "Did your dad ever apologize? Try to make amends for what he did?"

"My dad?" Incredulous, he stared back at her. "Apologize?"

Expecting Gus Langford to ever change would've been like asking the sun to set in the east. The man had gone to his grave without ever apologizing to anyone, as far as Devlin knew.

"You boys were not to blame for Heather's death. Betty probably told you that a hundred times, but I don't think any of you boys ever believed it. You were brainwashed by your dad."

He locked his gaze on hers and tried to make himself say the words she wanted to hear.

"Your father harped on that accident endlessly, blaming you boys and making sure you carried that guilt forever just to exonerate himself," she continued, tightening her grip on his hand. "Maybe he was too weak to face the truth, but he was the one behind the wheel when he backed over her. He was her father, and he should have been more careful."

"But—"

"None of you boys were even there, Dev. And none of you had been asked to watch her. Remember?"

"But we should have. Someone should have seen her follow him outside."

"You boys were doing *chores*. He was in a fit of temper over something and just stomped on the gas without watching out for her." She set her jaw, her gaze boring into his, as if she could change everything with the force of her will. "No matter what anyone says about big, tough, successful Gus Langford, he was harsh, he had a volatile temper and he was a weak man. A good one would've sheltered his sons, not tried to destroy them to assuage his own guilt. I just wish he were here right now so I could tell him so."

And she would have; he had no doubt of that. Even when just a bitty little thing, she'd stood up for Devlin at every opportunity, her hands jammed on her skinny hips, her jaw thrust out.

Though why she'd chosen him to be the brother she championed, he'd never figured out.

He stood up abruptly and started to clear the table, but she shook her head. "No need. Just wait while I put some of this food in containers for you. I'll never be able to eat it all."

"Really, you don't need to—"

"*Wait*. Don't move. You won't need to cook for a day,

and if you can give me some feedback on this meal, you'll be doing me a huge favor."

She'd grown up to be a pretty woman, but she still had her sass and spunk, and that same tender heart. Whoever married her would be very blessed indeed.

He blinked, blindsided by the random thought that had popped into his mind. When had *that* ever been a consideration? Not with her or anyone else.

He'd learned his lesson about risking his heart, over and over, each love and loss more painful than the last. And he'd resolved to never take that risk again.

Yeah, he'd certainly feared for her safety today and was relieved beyond measure that she was all right. And if he was totally honest with himself, *maybe* he even felt an unwanted glimmer of attraction. But now all he had to do was keep his distance and keep busy.

And in a few months, she'd be gone.

Chapter Nine

She'd looked forward to attending the quaint Pine Bend Community Church on Sunday morning. But with her first step out of bed, her ankle had buckled, sending a sharp burst of pain up her leg and a wave a dizziness through her.

After taking two ibuprofen, she'd spent the day in her cabin, with her foot propped on the coffee table in front of the sofa, while thumbing through her grandmother's recipes and writing extensive notes on possible adjustments. When that got too boring, she grabbed a spiral notebook and began listing possible scene edits for the novel she'd been mulling over.

Devlin didn't call or stop by all day, but after his abrupt departure Saturday night, she didn't expect to see him anytime soon, even though she'd sent the supper leftovers home with him, including the entire brown-sugar pound cake, plus the covered bowls of whipped cream and macerated strawberries that she'd made for dessert.

Someone with manners might've at least texted a thank-you for all of the food, and maybe some comments. He *knew* she wanted comments about the recipes she'd tried.

Then again she hadn't exactly been tactful when she'd lectured him about his father. She'd lectured a *Marine* as if he was ten years old. The thought made her cheeks burn even now. As much as she'd been trying to help, what grown man would want to hear about his father's litany of faults from someone who wasn't even family?

Her plan to use the next couple of months to push him into accepting more help for his hearing loss had probably just taken a giant step backward, and she only had herself to blame. But she wasn't a quitter, and at the next opportunity she might as well give it a shot. What did she have to lose?

By the next morning her ankle felt a little better, and both the dizziness and her headache had faded, so she withdrew some random cards from her grandma's recipe box and got to work in the kitchen. Something called aspic sounded…well, strange and jiggly, with vegetables suspended in gelatinized beef broth. *Ewww.* A hit in her grandmother's day, maybe. For millennial tastes, not so much.

Two dozen ways to prepare liver also got a boot to the back of the card file.

But Grandma's parmesan potato casserole and her coconut cloud cake showed definite promise, and Chloe did have all of the ingredients.

She'd just started scrubbing the potatoes when she heard someone knock on the screen door.

"It's just me—Dev. Can I bother you for a minute?"

His deep voice sent a little shiver of awareness through her, despite her renewed resolution to mind her own business from now on. "If you're bringing back food containers, just leave them on the porch," she called out as she dragged the vegetable peeler along the surface of a potato.

"If you're busy, I can come back, but I think you'll want to see this. I just got home from town and it's… kind of a present."

A present? From Devlin? Not likely. She rinsed off her hands and went to the door, still drying them with a paper towel…and pulled to a halt in shock.

Staring at her through the screen was a tall fluff ball of snowy-white, moth-eaten fur with a big red bow around its neck. Her heart melted. "Daisy?"

Devlin had clearly stayed to one side to let Daisy make her own introductions, but now he stepped into view. "It'll take a while for her coat to grow out, but the vet techs did a great job of cleaning her up, didn't they? They even found a bow."

Speechless, Chloe eased out of the door to avoid bumping Daisy and gently cradled her head between her hands.

She hadn't seemed this big when Chloe had first found her outside the cabin, but then she'd been a miserable, cowering pooch covered with matted hair and dirt. Now Chloe realized that the dog's head was level with her waist.

"You are a very big girl, and so beautiful," she murmured. She looked up at Devlin. "How long will it take for her to heal?"

"Probably six to twelve weeks, but she needs to go back in two to make sure she's healing correctly. She was so frantic with a neck cone that the vet decided she was better without it. We need to watch her to make sure she doesn't chew on her cast."

Chloe studied the bright green hard cast on the dog's leg. "Did the vet give you any other care instructions?"

"She needs to be confined in a small space and just go for short walks on a leash, only when necessary. No going up or down stairs, no running or play."

"So my cabin should be perfect, then."

"Actually, the vet said a dog crate was best, but Daisy's so big that I was thinking that she and I could spend a few nights in the tack room, just to get her acclimated."

"You'd sleep in the tack room?"

"In case she needs to go out or gets too agitated by the confinement. We don't really know what kind of life she's had before becoming a stray—or even if she's housebroken."

The offer touched Chloe's heart. She reached up to brush a kiss against his cheek. "That's so sweet of you."

Devlin seemed to wince a little at the "sweet." He cleared his throat. "Just practical. I'm almost always in the barn throughout the day, so I can take her outside then, too. You won't have to keep walking on a sore ankle."

"That's really kind. Thank you."

He turned to leave with the dog at his side, but then stopped. "By the way, the guys at the gas station had a good used tire—same brand as yours—and wheel that fits on your SUV. They put it on and then drove the vehicle out here this morning."

She felt a prick of guilt. She'd been disappointed when he didn't text a critique of the meal she'd sent home with him. Yet now she knew he'd been quietly busy on her behalf in more ways than one. "That was so kind of them—and you."

"Hope you don't mind that I told them to go ahead. Your phone went to voice mail, so I sent you a text and didn't hear back. They had some time first thing this morning, but otherwise they couldn't have done it until late tomorrow or even Wednesday."

So, apparently her phone was either on Mute or dead. "What do I owe you?"

"They put it on the ranch account." He shrugged. "We can figure it out later. Oh—and thanks for the great food yesterday. I'll drop off the containers later on."

"Any comments? Too much seasoning—or not enough?"

He thought for a moment, and then a half smile deepened the long slash of a dimple on one side of his lean, tanned face. "If I could only have one menu for the rest of my life and that was it, I would die a happy man."

"So it was all okay? Really?"

"Better than. The only problem is that I'll never remember how to pronounce the fancy name of that entrée, and I have no idea how to spell it."

"Boeuf bourguignon," she said, enunciating the name carefully. "I'll text you the name. Honestly, to pronounce it, I had to look it up on YouTube, and even there I found several ways to say it. So as long as you aren't in France and you come even close, people will probably know what you mean. Or just call it French beef stew."

Her heart warmed as she watched him carefully lift Daisy onto a pile of blankets in the back of his four-wheeler, touch the brim of his Stetson in farewell and then drive down the path toward the barns. The dog's white flag of a tail wagged happily as they disappeared from sight.

Dev's menu critique certainly wasn't the most in-depth and helpful she'd ever received, and it was probably laced with more charm than truth.

Yet he'd not only taken care of the ruined wheel on

her SUV, but gotten Daisy at the vet clinic, which was an incredibly thoughtful surprise. On top of that, he even planned to babysit the dog in the tack room, where the only place for him to sleep was a sofa far shorter than his six-plus feet.

She'd always thought of Dev as a reckless charmer; a wounded, self-destructive rebel who had crossed swords with his father at every opportunity, no matter the cost. A boy whose pain she'd felt clear to the depths of her bones—and who had surely needed her nurturing heart whether he knew it or not.

But whether it was due to maturity or the military, he'd become a different man over the years. Maybe he'd learned to mask his emotional scars. Maybe he'd simply buried them deep so he could finally forget. But either way she needed to stop underestimating the man he had become. And she also needed to guard her heart. It would be all too easy to fall deeply, irrevocably in love with a man like him—and maybe she already had. But she'd already learned her lesson on that score.

Loving someone had always just led to heartbreak, and she just couldn't take that risk again.

Figuring the injured dog would be uncomfortable and restless during the night despite her prescription pain pills, Devlin collected a thick stack of soft winter horse blankets and piled them in a corner of the tack room for a soft bed.

"Here you go, Daisy," he snapped his fingers and pointed to the makeshift bed, and the dog obediently hobbled over, awkwardly turned around a half dozen times and lay down. "Good girl."

Daisy watched him with pure devotion in her large,

liquid black eyes, her white plume of a tail thumping out a fervent thank-you against the blankets.

From beyond the closed tack-room door, Devlin could hear the sounds of the horses stirring in their stalls. The faint, distant bawling of the cattle as the herd moved away from the hay bunks and headed back out to the pasture. The call of a distant owl. Comforting sounds that could lull a man to sleep, without the interruption of gunfire or explosions.

Eyeing the club chairs and small sofa arranged around a cowhide in the center of the room—none of which would be useful as a bed for anyone past elementary school—he unrolled his sleeping bag and shook it out onto the cowhide on the floor. He settled down for the night. Not exactly the Ritz, though he'd had a lot worse. And with the miles he'd covered running on the trails north of the ranch, he ought to be tired enough to sleep.

But the blessed oblivion of sleep didn't come. Not until the wee hours, when he suddenly found himself facing off with the Dooley brothers again—only this time he was without a weapon of any kind, while they were both armed with an AK-47 out on the flat, arid high-desert expanses, with only knee-high sagebrush for cover.

Chloe was behind them, gagged and bound, unable to escape, her terrified gaze fixed on his as she silently begged for help.

His peripheral vision caught the approach of even more Dooley brothers, only now they were all in uniform, carrying military weapons and closing in from every side.

A deafening explosion to his right shook the ground. Threw bodies into the air. Shrapnel sliced through

smoke raining death and destruction in every direc-
tion. The terrible screams went on and on, threatening
to shatter his skull—

A soft, warm presence enveloped him. Slowed his
thundering heartbeat. Filled him with a sense of peace
and calm as it protected him from the horrors surrounding him…

He fought back the ragged cobweb edges of the
nightmare and slowly opened his eyes to find Daisy
pressed next to him, her massive white head on his
chest. Her gentle, knowing eyes were fixed on his, as
if she was trying to absorb his pain and offer comfort
in the only way she knew how.

For months he'd prayed for the end of the nightmares
that had ripped him from sleep, night after night. He'd
kept up those prayers until he'd finally realized that God
had better things to do and just wasn't going to listen.
And no wonder. Devlin had failed as a brother, son and
fiancé, and what he'd had to do as a soldier had haunted
his thoughts for years.

Surely he was beyond the possibility of forgiveness.
And even if God was willing, Dev would never be able
to forget, much less forgive himself.

Yet now, with this raggedy white dog lying close beside him, he felt…released from the horror somehow.
And somehow at greater peace. His eyes burned. He
drew in a jagged breath, his heart feeling just a little
less broken…if only for a little while.

And then he felt himself sinking deeper, deeper into
a dreamless, healing sleep.

Chapter Ten

If Daisy hadn't actually been the elderly hermit's service dog, then she possessed uncanny intuition and perception. Despite the hard, cold floor of the tack room and his thin sleeping bag, Devlin awoke more refreshed than he had in ages after a night with her comforting warmth pressed closely to his side.

After taking Daisy outside, he fed her, went to the main house to take care of the twins' puppy, then jogged up to the meadow for target practice and ran on the trails for a half hour. Already he could feel himself getting stronger, and he was doing better with the targets, slowly but surely. Afterward he stopped by his cabin for a quick shower and breakfast—the rest of the food Chloe had given him.

When he came back outside, Daisy was standing at his door, her wagging tail a blur of excitement at seeing him again. As if it had been years, not just an hour or so.

"How did you get up here so fast with that bum leg?" He ruffled the thick fur at her neck. "And how in the world did you escape?"

She pulled her lips back in a wide doggy grin and

wagged her tail even faster, her dark-eyed gaze riveted on his face.

He'd closed the tack-room door behind him; he was sure of that. "Doctor's orders—minimal exercise. Remember?"

He let her come into the cabin, stepped outside and closed the door behind him—firmly—and started jogging down the hill to get the four-wheeler for Daisy's trip back to the barn.

He hadn't gone a dozen yards before he heard her howling and frantically clawing at the door—which had to be worse for that fractured leg than a slow walk to the barn.

With a sigh, he went back up to the cabin and let her outside. "You, my dear, are high-maintenance."

She pressed against the side of his leg as they slowly descended the hill. She abruptly halted, her attention riveted on the trail ahead.

A moment later Chloe appeared at the junction of the trail and the path leading to her cabin, wearing a flour-dusted apron, with her hair pulled back into some sort of haphazard knot at her nape.

She couldn't have been dressed in a less flirtatious way, but for some strange reason she still looked so appealing that he wished he could walk right up to her and wrap his arms around her for a long embrace.

"I thought I heard Daisy howl," she said, eyeing the dog with obvious concern. "Isn't she supposed to be sedentary?"

"Tell her that. In fact maybe you can watch her while I get the four-wheeler. I thought she was locked in the tack room, but she escaped and followed me clear up to my cabin."

"Awww. She likes you," Chloe murmured, with a twinkle in her eye. "That's so cute."

"It's separation anxiety, more like it."

"Poor thing. If she did belong to that old guy, the trauma of him dying and leaving her all alone probably makes her afraid we'll disappear, too."

"Yeah. That must be it." He didn't want to bring up the other very plausible possibility—that the dog thought *he* was the one who needed attention and support, and was earnestly trying to do her job. "Well, she oughta like you well enough, so just keep her here for a few minutes, and I'll be right back."

Chloe nodded and took a firm grip on Daisy's collar with one hand and began stroking her, while crooning all sorts of singsong nonsense about her being a "wonderful dog" and a "big, beautiful girl."

He'd just rounded the first bend and stepped out of sight when Chloe yelled something that he couldn't quite decipher.

Pebbles started cascading down the slope from behind him.

A second later he heard the heavy panting and disjointed three-beat steps of a big dog running on three legs, trying to catch up.

He spun around just in time for Daisy to awkwardly barrel into him and knock him flat onto the trailside carpet of pine needles, under sixty-some pounds of wiggling dog, flailing paws and ecstatic slurps and kisses.

"I wasn't even gone *five minutes*, Daisy," he managed when he finally managed to push her gently away from him. "This has got to stop."

When the dog spun around and stared up the trail, he looked over his shoulder and saw Chloe standing a few feet away, her hands on her hips and her mouth twitching. "Need any help?"

"No. But once she regains all the weight she apparently lost, she's going to be dangerous."

"She certainly does like you best," Chloe said wistfully as she reached forward to offer him a hand up.

Just the touch of her hand in his sent warmth zipping up his arm, just like always.

"I'm really sorry she got away from me, but holding her back was like trying to stop a buffalo," Chloe added. "I did try to warn you."

A warning he hadn't heard.

Chloe crossed her arms over her chest and regarded him with a troubled look. "I know you don't want me to say it again. But it seems like you've just given up, and surely if you—"

He dusted off his jeans. "Just drop it. Okay?"

"No. Because there *has* to be something out there—now or maybe even in the future—that can help. A new device, a new surgery technique. A better hearing aid. A different clinic somewhere. Your life could be in danger someday because you didn't hear a warning. And what if someone screamed for help? What then?"

He gritted his teeth, wanting to ignore her. To ignore everything that made him feel damaged and less of the person he'd been. His identity as an effective warrior had literally gone up in smoke, and he doubted that he would ever find a way to accept it. "I was told. By *experts*. Hearing aids help somewhat for now, but eventually they probably won't."

"Look—I'm only trying to help." She hesitated for a split second, and then her hands moved swiftly. *How will you communicate if and when your hearing fails?*

Please let me help you while I'm here. It'll be easier to learn while you can hear the spoken words...

He wanted to turn and walk away. But she was still watching him, quietly waiting, and he finally gave up. *I...know some*, he signed laboriously, thinking about each movement of his hands. *Satisfied?*

Her eyes opened wide and a joyful smile lit up her face. *That's fantastic! So now we can start practicing, and it will bring everything back for you—*

He held up a hand and shook his head. "Thanks, but no," he said aloud. "It could be years before I need it. I may never need to sign at all."

"That isn't what you just said. You said—"

"If you'll excuse me, I need to get to work."

He was walking into the barn a few minutes later, when his cellphone vibrated. *Anyone but Chloe, please.* He grabbed it from his pocket, relief flooding through him when he read the caller ID. "Hey, Jess. How's the trip?"

There was a long, static-filled pause, and then Jess said something Devlin couldn't hear. He turned up the conversation volume on his amplified phone to the highest level. "What?"

"Mostly good. Abby visited some colleges and chose one. The visit with Lindsey was rocky—she didn't pay much attention to the twins and seemed distracted and impatient. Her attention was mostly riveted on her cell phone."

Lindsey had visited the ranch once while Devlin and his brothers were growing up, and that news didn't surprise him one bit. "How did the girls take it?"

"Not too well. They were nervous about seeing her again—but I think they were also imagining it would be a big, happy reunion."

"Poor kids."

"The social worker had thought a visit would be a good idea, but it'll be a long while before we try that again. Maybe not until they're much older. So, how's everything at home?"

"Good enough."

"The girls keep asking about Poofy."

"He's fine. Tell them that I let him outside every couple of hours during the day and we play fetch. You're coming home tomorrow, right?"

"Actually, no. Planned on it, but we heard about a promising stallion prospect near Sacramento, so we're going to swing by and check him out. We should be back Thursday—or Friday at the latest."

Devlin closed his eyes. *Great.*

"Dev—are you still there?"

"Yeah—that's fine. Thursday or Friday."

"So, how are you and the new renter getting along?"

"Uh…okay."

Devlin could hear some indistinguishable voices in the background, and then Jess came back to the phone. "Grandma Betty wants to know if you've been friendly and if you've been trying to help Chloe feel at home. I can't imagine why she'd feel the least bit of doubt, though. Can you?"

Devlin heard an undercurrent of laughter in his brother's voice. "Nope."

"That's it? Just no? Grandma is behind me, demanding a full report, so give me a little more or she'll take my phone and you'll be on this call for an hour."

That was the truth. Grandma Betty would want to know what he'd had for breakfast, lunch and dinner, and if he was getting enough sleep, plus every last de-

Get Up To 4 Free Books!

Dear Reader,

IT'S A FACT: if you answer 4 quick questions, we'll send you 4 FREE REWARDS from each series you try!

Try **Love Inspired® Romance Larger-Print** books featuring Christian characters facing modern-day challenges.

Try **Love Inspired® Suspense Larger-Print** novels featuring Christian characters facing challenges to their faith... and lives

Or **TRY BOTH!**

I'm not kidding you. As a leading publisher of women's fiction, we value your opinions... and your time. That's why we are prepared to reward you handsomely for completing our mini-survey. In fact, we have 4 Free Rewards for you, including 2 free books and 2 free gifts from each series you try!

Thank you for participating in our survey,

Pam Powers

To get your 4 FREE REWARDS:
Complete the survey below and return the insert today to receive up to 4 FREE BOOKS and FREE GIFTS guaranteed!

"4 for 4" MINI-SURVEY

1 Is reading one of your favorite hobbies?
☐ YES ☐ NO

2 Do you prefer to read instead of watch TV?
☐ YES ☐ NO

3 Do you read newspapers and magazines?
☐ YES ☐ NO

4 Do you enjoy trying new book series with FREE BOOKS?
☐ YES ☐ NO

Please send me my Free Rewards, consisting of **2 Free Books from each series I select** and **Free Mystery Gifts**. I understand that I am under no obligation to buy anything, as explained on the back of this card.

❏ **Love Inspired® Romance Larger-Print** (122/322 IDL GNPV)
❏ **Love Inspired® Suspense Larger-Print** (107/307 IDL GNPV)
❏ **Try Both** (122/322/107/307 IDL GNP7)

FIRST NAME	LAST NAME

ADDRESS

APT.#	CITY

STATE/PROV.	ZIP/POSTAL CODE

READER SERVICE—Here's how it works:

▲ If offer card is missing write to: Reader Service, P.O. Box 1341, Buffalo, NY 14240-8531 or visit www.ReaderService.com ▲

BUSINESS REPLY MAIL
FIRST-CLASS MAIL   PERMIT NO. 717   BUFFALO, NY

POSTAGE WILL BE PAID BY ADDRESSEE

READER SERVICE
PO BOX 1341
BUFFALO NY 14240-8571

NO POSTAGE
NECESSARY
IF MAILED
IN THE
UNITED STATES

tail about her favorite little redhead, whom she'd doted on years ago.

"Chloe's fine and as bossy as ever. I mostly try to stay out of her way, but like I told you before, that hasn't been working out too well." He thought for a moment, then decided to skip the Dooley incident, at least for now. *And* the long embrace and kiss afterwards, which still had the power to warm him from head to toe whenever he thought about it…which was mostly 24/7. "For a ranch this big, it's surprising to see how often I end up running into her. And then there's her dog…"

As if Daisy knew she'd been mentioned, she looked up at Devlin with adoring eyes, took an awkward step and stumbled into him. He grabbed at a tree branch just in time to stop his fall into a pile of boulders beside the trail.

"Her dog?"

"It's the size of a mastodon, but that's a long story. Just know that there'll be one ex-Marine who'll be very happy the day you decide to come home."

Devlin was the most stubborn, irritating person on the planet, Chloe thought to herself, fuming as she took the trash out to the bear-proof container next to the main trail in front of her cabin.

Despite her nagging headache, she'd spent the rest of her day working in the kitchen and starting the first draft of the introduction for her cookbook, but her thoughts kept veering back to Devlin despite her resolution to not think of him at all.

Why did he not listen to reason?

Wouldn't it be easier to become proficient at sign language while he still had enough hearing to associate verbal communication with sign? Wouldn't it be *logical* for him to take advantage of any opportunity to improve his skills?

If he had any sense, he would pay attention to her.

Like the wounded animals she'd helped rehabilitate back to healthy life, she knew he could lead a more full and abundant life if he'd just accept the help he needed. That he would choose denial over progress baffled her.

Not that she was an expert by any means. It had been years since she'd used sign language to communicate with Grandma Lydia. But she could start watching You-Tube videos to tune up her own skills, and then she'd be ready when he finally realized she was right.

And if he never did—being a stubborn Langford, that was a strong possibility—she could save all of those links for him in an email and he could just do it on his own if he ever wised up.

She turned toward her cabin and started back up the path, but her legs suddenly felt rubbery, her muscles weak. She blinked as black spots seemed to dance in front of her eyes.

The path ahead lengthened into a long, dim tunnel. The cabin door seemed to be a million miles away as she made herself take just one more step…then another. *Please, Lord, not now.*

With Devlin staying with Daisy in the tack room for the next few nights, he wouldn't be passing by on his way to the last cabin.

So she was all alone.

Chapter Eleven

Devlin dismounted, hooked the nearside stirrup over the saddle horn and loosened the cinch a few notches, then glanced at the big tack room window that looked out into the indoor arena.

A vague sense of uneasiness settled in his midsection.

This was his last ride for the day, and he'd found himself checking that window every so often to see if Chloe had come yet to watch for a while. She usually did at the end of the afternoon and would then slip away…probably reminiscing about the years when she'd been a little girl watching her dad work horses in this same arena.

Dev had come to look forward to seeing her at the window. But after their argument this morning, she'd probably decided she had much better things to do.

He always ended his rides with a long cooldown at a walk, working each horse through slow figure eights, side passes and backing up, reinforcing a quiet, relaxed attitude under saddle. Now he led the paint gelding out of the arena and into the barn, crosstied him and glanced at the front door of the barn, half expecting to see Chloe walk in.

Strange.

He hadn't seen her go by on her daily jog. She hadn't dropped by with something she'd just taken warm from the oven. Her SUV hadn't moved.

Surely she was just fine and hard at work, yet a small inner voice whispered to him. *Go. You need to check.*

As soon as he had the colt unsaddled and put away, he took Daisy for a short walk, went up to the house to let the twins' pup out into the fenced yard and then he jogged up the trail leading to the cabins on the pretext of going after something he'd forgotten.

As he passed by, he'd probably see Chloe through her large cabin windows, working in her kitchen. But at least he'd know she was all right.

He slowed as he neared her cabin, surprised to see that the screen door was wide open. When would she ever leave it ajar like that, a welcome mat for the chipmunks that scurried endlessly around the cabins in search of food?

He knocked on the door, called her name and then walked inside. "Chloe?"

No answer.

It took just a moment to search the place, and then he spun around and went back outside.

Chloe.

She'd been hidden from view on his way up to the cabin. But now he could see her slumped against a log well off the path to one side, in the lee of a cluster of boulders.

"Chloe?" He reached her in a heartbeat. Knelt at her side and touched her shoulder. "What happened? Did you fall?"

"No… I just felt a little woozy for a moment."

"Did you pass out?"

She frowned a little. "No."

"Should I call for an ambulance?"

At that she looked up at him in alarm. "Goodness, *no*."

Still, she appeared ashen, and her skin felt cool and clammy when he touched her forehead. He hadn't noticed for several days—maybe she'd masked it with makeup—but now he could see the fading remnants of the bruise she'd incurred during her altercation with the Dooleys last Saturday.

"Have you been having headaches? Dizziness?"

She didn't answer, but he caught that same old stubborn glint in her eyes before her gaze skated away, and his suspicion grew stronger. She'd adamantly refused to go to the ER that day, but now he wished he'd somehow managed to take her anyway.

"I've seen a number of fellow soldiers who suffered concussions, and I'm guessing you might have one. You should see a doctor."

Her chin lifted slightly. "No."

"Just to make *sure* you're okay."

She glanced at him, then looked away. "I admit… I did bang my head a little on Saturday. But I looked up the symptoms of a concussion on the internet and this is nothing, I'm sure of it."

He studied her for a moment. "And yet you were dizzy just now. If you'd passed out and hit your head on one of these rocks, we wouldn't even be having this discussion."

The thought made his blood run cold.

"I'm already better," she continued, with an airy wave of her hand. She sat up straighter, "Thanks for the concern, but I'll be fine."

She wanted him to walk away? Was she kidding?

"Actually, I think I'll stay for a few minutes, if you don't mind."

They sat together for another twenty minutes, watching a trio of chipmunks chase each other around the foundation of the cabin as the sun started to sink behind the mountains to the west. He'd forgotten how beautiful and peaceful this place was, with the sweet smell of pine in the air and a breeze sighing through the branches overhead.

He reached over and took her hand in his. "Okay—now tell me the truth. Everything. Or I'm not leaving."

"I admit... I've had a mild headache since the Dooley situation. And there've been a couple of times when I've felt a little woozy," she muttered after a long silence. "But I don't want to talk about it. Does that sound familiar?"

At that he cracked a smile. *"Touché."*

She tilted her head, her gaze fixed on his. "I just had a little fall. No big deal. But your hearing is a lot more serious. What if you can't hear an urgent warning, or you miss hearing something you absolutely need to know?"

He clenched his jaw.

"Not that I want to interfere or anything, but I don't think you've done all you could do to make your life better. Just sayin'."

Typical Chloe. Practically on death's door one minute, and the next, trying to help him whether he wanted her to or not.

But he was so relieved to have her alert, talking and back to worrying about him, that all he could do was drape an arm around her shoulders to pull her closer to his side. He brushed a kiss against her temple.

When they finally rose, he grinned down at her and

gently cradled her face between his hands. "No more falls, bumps or fainting. Understand? I honestly don't know what I'd do if you weren't around to tell me what to do."

And then he drew her close for a kiss to convey just how much he meant it.

Despite Daisy's warm, comforting presence, Devlin stayed wide awake until midnight, his thoughts spinning in endless circles before he finally drifted off to sleep.

He'd been blindsided by what he'd felt when he found Chloe nearly unconscious outside her cabin, and by the realization of what her loss would mean to him. Then blindsided by the effect of that kiss.

But that wasn't possible.

He couldn't have any real feelings for her beneath the prickly aspects of their relationship over the years.

He'd resolved long ago to never again be responsible for anyone besides himself. Never again risk *loving* someone, because he knew that love only led to grief and heartbreak—every single time. That had been his mantra ever since Gina died.

Yet there'd never been anyone in his life quite like Chloe, and now he was beginning to realize just how much he was going to miss her when she left. He almost wished he dared to take one more chance.

But she deserved a far better man than him.

She wasn't going to miss Devlin when her time in Montana was up. Not. One. Bit. How could he be so... so *stubborn*?

She'd seen that quiet smile of his when she'd tried to talk sense into him after her little episode yesterday evening, and now she knew that he would never change.

So be it.

He'd apparently managed just fine before she came along, and he could just bumble along on his own after she left. And if he proved to be too aggravating, too distracting, she and Daisy could always leave Montana early.

A flashback from the incident with the Dooley brothers slammed into her thoughts. Fear lanced through her as she relived the moment they'd hit her left rear bumper with their truck, sending her SUV careening off the shoulder of the highway.

She would never forget their avid expressions as they sauntered toward her.

Eager. Self-satisfied with their success at cornering their prey. And they'd looked absolutely remorseless. She had no doubt that they would have been without mercy if they had caught her.

A deep shudder shook her as she slid a loaf pan of Grandma Lydia's almond, cranberry and white-chocolate bread into the oven, set the timer on the stove, and braced her shaking hands on the counter.

If she was still this rattled over her near-miss experience, how did someone ever get over their terror if no one arrived to rescue them? If they had to live with the memory of that nightmare every single day?

She'd been so incredibly blessed when Devlin had shown up just in time—like Superman, Batman and a gunslinger from the Wild West all rolled into one, despite his damaged shoulder and weakened right arm.

A true hero. A surprising layer to a complex man with a troubled past.

She'd always worried about him—knowing he'd reveled in wild parties as a teen, imagining he might still be that person. Or worse. Fearing that he could end up exactly like her alcoholic father, who had managed to hide his addiction so well. *Most* of the time.

Her cheeks started to burn. Whatever he was or wasn't, he'd come to save her, and she hadn't even thought to ask him if dealing with the Dooleys had injured his shoulder even further. Instead she'd chosen to harass him once again about his hearing issue and medical care—which was not her business at all.

A sense of guilt crawled through her. What had she been thinking?

There was a big difference between being caring and concerned, and being an obnoxious, bossy pest.

She grabbed a zester, scraped it across the surface of a fresh, fragrant orange with a vengeance, until it was bare, and then halved the orange and squeezed all of the juice. After adding the juice and orange zest to the sugar she'd measured into a saucepan, she put the pan on the stove and began to idly stir.

Maybe she could bring this warm loaf of bread to him as a peace offering and apologize, with a promise that she would stop trying to interfere with his life. In fact she could promise to stay out of his way completely. The poor man deserved that small courtesy, at the very least.

Even though he'd apparently stolen the heart of her traitorous new dog.

After running in the early morning hours and lifting weights, Devlin did the chores. He was headed to the main house, with Daisy at his side, when he saw Chloe coming down the trail from her cabin. She no longer favored her left ankle, he realized. And she was bearing something oblong in a plastic bag that just might be delicious. He sure hoped so.

"I was hoping I would catch you in time. Maybe you'd like this with your supper or breakfast tomorrow." She handed him the package. "This is Grandma Lydia's almond, cranberry and white-chocolate quick bread, with an orange glaze."

The citrus aroma wafting into the air was amazing.

"One slice is missing," she added, shooting him a quick, tentative smile. "I had to do a taste test. I wasn't too sure about the orange glaze with the white chocolate, but I actually think Grandma hit this one out of the park. You'll let me know what you think, right? I... um...enclosed a little questionnaire this time. To make it easier."

"Thanks." He thought about sitting alone at the big oak table in that big, empty house, with just two dogs for company. "Do you want to join me for supper? Nothing fancy—I'm just nuking a frozen meal and there are plenty more in the freezer."

"Thanks, but... I should probably get home." A faint pink blush slipped into her cheeks. "I've been thinking, though. And I need to apologize."

He raised an eyebrow, mystified. "For what?"

"From our first meeting here, I said I was going to mind my own business and stay out of your way."

That prospect no longer seemed as appealing as it had at first. "I don't know that it's imperative, Chloe."

She gave a firm shake of her head. "You saved me from those despicable Dooleys and came to my rescue again yesterday evening, because you were concerned. And for that I thank you from the bottom of my heart. But... I haven't been so kind in return, constantly lecturing you about taking care of yourself better. So I promise to stop." She bit her lower lip. "Though honestly, you *really* do need to listen, because..."

Her voice trailed off and a faint, rueful smile tugged at the corner of her mouth. "Sorry."

"How are you feeling today? Is everything all right?"

"Yes. Of course. Perfectly fine."

He studied her more closely. There were fine lines of tension bracketing her mouth. "Really? No headaches at all? They can last for months after a concussion."

She hitched a shoulder. "Well…maybe a little."

"Then why not just admit it?"

"Because I don't want to. In your teens and twenties, you feel young and invincible. Then a little health problem crops up and you realize that you're not."

"I know," he said quietly.

Her eyes widened with instant regret. "Of course you do. Sorry. I can be so utterly tactless sometimes."

Her gaze fell on Daisy, and a look of pure longing crossed her face that she quickly hid. "How is she doing?"

As usual, Daisy was at his side, pressed against his leg. He looked down at her and ruffled the thick fur at her neck. "She hasn't gnawed on her cast yet, she seems to be well housebroken and she eats like a horse."

"You must have an incredible knack with animals. She already seems totally devoted to you."

"But she's still your dog. Whenever you feel ready to keep her at your cabin, I'll bring her up."

"How could I do that?" Chloe gave him a doubtful look. "From watching her, I think that would be cruel. She's exactly where she wants to be. With you."

"It's not what you think."

He could just leave it at that, the easier way out, and let Chloe believe the dog liked him best because he was the more wonderful human being.

Or he could tell her the humiliating truth and reveal

a weak part of himself that he'd refused to share with anyone else.

"Well...have a good evening." Chloe turned toward the trail leading up to the cabins.

"Wait, Chloe. Please." He tipped his head toward the house and its covered, wrap-around porch filled with a half dozen rockers, wooden chairs and a wide porch swing, all fitted with colorful cushions. "Can you join me for a minute?"

She hesitated, then followed him up the steps and settled into a white wooden rocker.

He took a chair facing hers, and Daisy sat next to him with her head in his lap. "It isn't that this dog likes me best. I think she assumes I'm her job."

Chloe's eyes flared wider. "What?"

"Not in the guard dog or herding sense. I've been thinking about that old codger who had a service dog, and Daisy just has to be the one. The vet said he was a loner, and given his age, he had probably served in Vietnam. Maybe he dealt with PTSD, and she was trained as a therapy dog. Or maybe she learned by instinct. But she has definitely done it before."

"Ahhh. That makes sense. What a great dog! I suppose she was a wonderful..." her voice trailed off and her eyes filled with compassion as his words registered. "Oh."

"It's ironic, really." He looked beyond Chloe to the rugged, snowcapped mountains to the west. "I was encouraged to accept a service dog, but even the offer seemed humiliating and I refused. I figured it was a sign of weakness and that I should handle everything on my own. Here I was, a grown man. A big, tough Marine and all that. How could a dog possibly help?"

She watched him, silently waiting for him to continue.

He set his jaw. "I do fine these days, really. I don't need anyone or anything to…"

Apparently sensing his defensiveness and abrupt change of mood, Daisy nudged him.

He looked down at her and recognized the automatic lie for what it was. Fear.

Fear of failure, of loss, of measuring up. Everything that had been instilled in him since he was a kid on this ranch, and then exacerbated by the explosion that stole his military career.

Even beyond that he'd already lost so much. The thought of facing the eventual loss of a beloved service dog was more than he'd dared to contemplate. So he'd refused the offer…and now he knew he'd made a mistake.

"I am doing better," he added after a long pause. "I rarely have flashbacks, and the nightmares don't come as often. Though when they hit, the night is totally lost for any chance of sleep, and the next day I'm in a daze. Useless."

"And Daisy?"

"She proved me wrong," he said simply, resting a hand on her shoulders, her warmth and soft fur reassuring even now. "I made her a soft dog bed in the corner of the tack room the first night she was with me. When a nightmare hit, she crawled over and rested her head on my chest, as if she knew what to do. Her presence changed everything. I can't explain it, really. A subconscious awareness of a protector, in case an enemy strikes? It doesn't make sense, I suppose. There are no enemies here. But she seems to sense my agitation and then she comes over to lay right next to me. She thinks I'm her job. And…well, it helps."

"That's wonderful, Dev."

He nodded. "With her in the room, I ended up sleeping better than I have in a long, long time. And last night too, once I got to sleep. I think I'll move back to my cabin tonight and bring her with me, unless you want her with you now. She's definitely housebroken, so you shouldn't have any problems."

"I'm so glad to hear it's working out well, Dev." Chloe leaned forward and put her hand over his. "This will be just perfect. I think it was meant to be, and really, you are doing me a great favor."

"What?"

"I felt so awful for her when she showed up at my door. There was nothing I wanted more than to help her. But I honestly don't know where I'll be living in Kansas City, and finding places that allow big dogs is almost impossible. I'm relieved to know she'll have a good home with you."

He blinked. "Wait—"

She gave him a cheery smile that seemed to wobble a bit at the edges as she stood. "I've got bread rising on the counter, so I'd better get back to my cabin. Have a great night. Both of you."

She'd seemed sad and wistful over Daisy, and he'd only wanted to reassure her that the dog was still hers. So where had the conversation gone off the rails? Had she just sacrificed a dog she wanted badly, just to make him happy?

Knowing Chloe, that shouldn't be a surprise.

He watched her head up the trail to her cabin, then looked down at Daisy and cradled her broad head between his hands.

"I'm not sure about what just happened, but we'll get it figured out. One way or another, you've got yourself a forever home."

The wonderful aroma rising from the package of bread was so tempting that he rose and took it into the kitchen, with Daisy at his heels. "What do you think—should we give this a try?"

The twins' pup romped over to sit next to Daisy as soon as he cut a slice of the moist golden-brown loaf. "Second thoughts. I'm not sure about the nuts and white chocolate for dogs. I think you and your little buddy would be better off having a dog biscuit instead."

He tossed a biscuit to each of them, and then sampled a slice of the bread. He closed his eyes and savored another bite…and suddenly it was gone. "Wow. That gets an A+ from me. Easy review."

He pulled a folded sheet of paper—make that *several* sheets—from the plastic bag.

Apparently he'd failed in his previous reviews of Chloe's baking experiments, because this time she'd left nothing to chance. She'd typed up a list of twenty questions, complete with a numbered set of directions at the top.

He scanned the questions and couldn't help but laugh. He had no idea what even half of the technical baking terms meant.

Only Chloe—with her endless determination and sweetly earnest enthusiasm—could come up with a veritable term paper for evaluating a loaf of bread.

Chapter Twelve

Chloe awoke the next morning to the sound of small fists beating on her cabin door and the sound of excited chatter.

"We weren't 'spose to come this early. Grandma Betty said so."

"Did not. She said at breakfast, and right now it's breakfast time."

"She's gonna be mad, and so is Uncle Jess. You wait and see." A little voice harrumphed in displeasure. "And it will be *all your fault*!"

This had to be the twins, Chloe thought as she reached for her robe and slippers and headed for the door.

Sure enough, there were two kindergarten-size blondes on the step. "Good morning, girls. How are you?"

Both of their mouths dropped open when they looked up at her, and then they looked at each other. "I *told* you we'd wake her up, Bella. She still has jammies on."

A young woman appeared on the path to the cabin, coming at a dead run, her long blond hair escaping a haphazard bun at her nape. She pulled to a breathless stop next to the girls and rested a firm hand on each of them.

"I am so, so sorry. We got home late last night, and I told them to wait to come see you until later, but they snuck off. I'm afraid they've been very excited about a new person staying here." She extended a hand. "I'm Abby Halliday, and you must be Chloe."

"Correct." Chloe accepted her brief, warm handshake. "And really, the girls were no bother at all."

Abby gave her a wry smile. "Since we're all here, let me introduce Bella and Sophie. And yes—they are identical, which can be a challenge at first. But now Sophie wants shorter hair, so that helps people who don't see them often."

Chloe grinned down at the girls. "I'm delighted to meet you both."

Bella gave her a doubtful look. "Grandma Betty said you have curly *red* hair."

"I did. But it got darker when I grew up," Chloe said. "Did you know that I lived here when I was your age? My daddy worked on this ranch for five years. Then we moved away."

Bella nodded solemnly. "We came two Christmases ago. But we get to stay forever and ever 'cause we got 'dopted."

"Momma didn't want us," Sophie whispered, her eyes downcast.

Abby drew in a sharp breath and briefly closed her eyes. "No, sweetheart. It wasn't like that. She still loves you. But she can't take care of you, so she wanted you to have a good, permanent home here with us. With ponies and puppies and people who also love you. Remember?"

"Sounds like you two are very blessed." Chloe smiled at the girls and then raised her gaze to meet

Abby's. "Can I invite you all in? I can make you breakfast, if you'd like."

"Actually, Betty hopes you'll come down to the big house and join us all. She said she'll have breakfast ready in an hour." Abby grinned. "She said to tell you that she's making your favorites—but she wouldn't tell me what they are."

"I can't even guess what she means, because everything she's ever made was wonderful. I'll be there."

"Excellent. Oh—and by the way, Dev told us that you're busy with some projects. I promise I'll try hard to make sure the twins won't be a nuisance in the future."

"We just wanted to see if she had cookies." Sophie's rosebud mouth formed a pout and her big blue eyes shimmered. "Like Uncle Devlin told us about last night."

The girls were so adorable that Chloe wanted to hug them both and promise them the moon, just to see them smile. "No cookies yet this morning, I'm afraid. But when I make them, I promise to bring you some. What kind do you like best?"

The girls exchanged looks.

"Nooo raisins." Bella made a face. "They're *yucky.*"

"And not dark ones."

"I believe Sophie means molasses cookies, though I'm sure they'll be very polite and will appreciate anything you make, and won't be particular. Right, girls?"

They nodded, looking so crestfallen as Abby herded them toward the trail that Chloe could barely suppress a chuckle.

Grandma Lydia had known her stuff when it came to grandkids and cookies, she remembered fondly.

Wonderful sugar cookies with a heavy dusting of sparkly, colorful sugar on top. Fudgy chocolate crackle cookies. Tender, buttery shortbread wonders that melted in one's mouth. And of course the cookies Devlin loved—chocolate chip, which could be made with M&M's instead.

Abby glanced at the clock as she went back inside. An hour was plenty of time to get at least one batch made. It never hurt to make a good first impression— even with little girls. *And maybe with Devlin...*

She firmly dismissed the thought. He clearly wasn't interested. Maybe he was still grieving the loss of his girlfriend, and maybe he always would. And even if he eventually healed, *she* definitely wasn't interested. That last debacle in Minneapolis had cured her of taking foolish chances.

So why did that sneaky little inner voice in her head keep insisting that she was wrong?

Chloe knocked on the back door of the main house an hour later, suddenly feeling a little self-conscious.

She'd spent her life being wary about anyone who seemed to have a proclivity for drinking. But now it struck her that others might look at her and wonder the same thing. Would they think she was like her father?

It had been eighteen years since she and Dad had packed up and left without so much as a goodbye. She'd never had any doubt as to why they had to leave—the same thing had happened at other ranches before and after their five years with the Langfords.

But the lure of the bottle had always outweighed any responsibility to his family and job. And though Dad could hold his liquor and hide the truth surprisingly well, every ranch owner found out sooner or later and sent him packing. Just one of things she'd never been able to forgive, despite the words of the Lord's Prayer she recited every night.

But she hadn't come here wanting to deal with her past or to insert herself into the lives of the people here. She'd simply looked forward to seeing Betty and Jess, and wanted a chance to work on her writing in peaceful isolation.

Now she just had to get through this breakfast and be sociable to everyone who had come home last night. Then she could go back to her cabin, get to work and hope everyone would leave her in peace.

She heard small footsteps racing across the kitchen to the door.

"I can do it!"

"No, me!"

"Abbeeee!" one of the girls wailed. "Bella hit me."

"Manners, girls," Abby said quietly as she opened the door wide and gave them a stern look. "Go wash up for breakfast. Now. And, Bella, you need to put on a clean shirt."

The twins raced out of the kitchen and Abby smiled at Chloe. "Come on in, if you dare. As you've already seen, the little hooligans are a little overexcited. They were up way past their bedtime last night and awoke too early."

Chloe walked inside and handed her a plastic-bag-covered paper plate filled with a towering dome of M&M's cookies. "These are for...whenever. The bag isn't sealed yet because they're still a bit warm."

"Wow. They look and smell amazing." Abby turned and hid them on top of the fridge. "I've already heard a lot about your cooking, and I can see Dev is right."

Devlin had already been talking about her? What on earth had he been saying? "Um...thanks. I think."

"Oh, it was all good, believe me. He says you're an excellent cook. Feel free to stop by anytime you feel like sharing what you've baked."

Abby went to the stove to pull out a breakfast casserole and set it on a trivet, then pulled out a second pan of caramel-pecan cinnamon rolls.

Abby studied the food arranged on the kitchen counter. "We've got orange rolls, mixed fresh fruit, a platter of crispy hash brown patties, juice, coffee and…hmm. Oh, yes, maple sausage."

"Wow. This is enough for an army." Chloe looked around the room. "Where's Betty? Isn't she here?"

"She was up early and insisted on making everything. Then she went to lie down for a while because her hip was aching. She's improved a lot since her hip replacement in November, but the long drive home yesterday didn't do her much good, I'm afraid."

Betty's hair had been silver years ago, so how old was she now? Chloe felt a little catch in her heart, wishing she'd come for visits through the years. "Is she in good health?"

"Oh, my." Abby laughed. "Very much so. She turned seventy-eight last month and don't even *think* of referring to her as elderly, or she'll be highly offended. In fact we had a little incident here with a hired hand, late last fall. She grabbed her rifle and helped me subdue him until Jess and a deputy arrived. It was like seeing a five-foot John Wayne in a pink housecoat."

Chloe grinned. "Sounds like she hasn't changed a bit."

"Still tough as shoe leather, and planning to live till I'm 110," Betty chortled as she limped through the kitchen doorway. She beamed at Chloe as she moved forward to envelop her in a long, grandmotherly hug,

then stepped back to look at her, head to toe. "My goodness, you've grown into such a beautiful young lady! I
can't believe my eyes. It's wonderful to see you again."

Jess and Devlin came in through the back door with
Daisy at their heels, hung their Stetsons on the nearby
rack and shucked off their boots.

Devlin tipped his head in a silent greeting to Chloe,
but Jess strode across the kitchen to give her a hug.
"Good to see you again, kid. I hope you had a good trip
and didn't have any trouble with my brother while we
were gone. He can be mighty surly."

Both brothers were tall, with near-black hair and
beautiful silver-blue eyes, framed by long, thick lashes
any woman would envy. But in Jess, she could see what
Devlin might look like without the emotional and physical ravages of war. Her heart wrenched. "He…he was
most kind."

"Dev? Kind?" Jess shot a look of amazement at his
brother and gave him a playful nudge with his elbow.
"That'd be a first."

"Boys," Betty said without heat. "Get washed up so
we can say grace."

The twins quickly vied for the chairs on either side
of Devlin and looked up at him with adoring eyes.

He grinned down at them and whispered something
that made them laugh. Then Bella wiggled in her chair
and knocked her plastic cup over, sending milk flying
all over her pink T-shirt and Devlin's lap.

Her eyes instantly filled with tears and her lower
lip trembled. "Sorry, Uncle Devlin. I-I didn't mean to."

"It was my fault, sweetie. No big deal." He curved
an arm around her thin shoulders for a quick, reassuring hug. "Only the Wicked Witch has trouble with getting wet. We'll dry."

Chloe stared at him, surprised. He'd been career military until his accident and had no kids as far as she knew. So when had he become so adept at calming a child? Her heart warmed at his gentleness—another surprising layer to the man who had grown and matured into someone she barely knew.

Once everyone was sitting around the long oak table in the kitchen, Betty swung her stern gaze around the table, landing on Devlin until he joined hands with the rest of them.

"Dear Lord, we thank you for our many blessings. For bringing Devlin safely home to us from his military service, for bringing Chloe to us once again. Thank you for watching over us throughout our travels and for enriching our lives as we come together as family once more. We ask that you watch over Tate and keep him safe, and bless Jess and Abby as they begin their wedding plans. And, Lord, watch over our girls as they finish their last two months in kindergarten. Finally, thank you for your bounty and this meal before us. Amen."

Following a chorus of amens, everyone began passing around the bowls and platters of food, while Abby brought a coffeepot and pitcher of juice to the table and began to pour.

Betty tapped the side of her glass to still the twins' chatter. "Now, everyone remember—Easter is this Sunday. So make sure you are all set the night before." She looked at the girls with a stern expression, though her eyes were twinkling and she barely managed to hold back a smile. "That means no lost shoes, no dress changes at the last minute. And *no* stomping in mud puddles on the way to the car. That goes for Devlin and Jess, as well. We don't want to be late."

The twins giggled. "They don't have dresses, Grandma," they said in unison.

"They did love mud puddles when they were your age, though. And they were forever losing their good church shoes."

Grinning, Abby leaned close to Chloe as she passed a platter of orange rolls. "I wasn't here then, but apparently it was quite a zoo. I hear that one Sunday, they made it just in time for the final hymn."

"I wasn't here when they were that young, but I believe it." Chloe passed the cinnamon rolls, wishing she could polish off an entire roll drenched in thick caramel. But even her most conservative guess on the carb content landed it far beyond anything she could try to adjust for at this meal.

Life was definitely unfair.

"What is Tate doing these days?" she asked as she took a serving spoon of the mixed fruit and passed the bowl to her left. The youngest of the Langford brothers had been the most playful of the three, an endless tease with a wicked sense of humor, at least until their sister's death. "Is he still in Montana?"

Jess shook his head. "We don't see him much. He follows the rodeo circuit, year after year. He only shows up when he breaks something and comes home to heal up for a while."

Betty harrumphed. "That foolish boy needs to find the right woman and settle down before he does something to himself that the docs can't fix."

Apparently Tate was a touchy subject.

"So, how was your trip?" Chloe asked to no one in particular.

Abby smiled. "The girls enjoyed every minute at

Disneyland, of course. We had two full days there, and the crowds weren't very heavy."

"We went on the It's a Small World ride three times," Jess said grimly. "The girls loved it, but that song has been running through my head ever since."

"You're a good man, Jess. They'll always remember going on that ride with you," Betty said with a twinkle in her eye. She took a sip of her coffee. "After Disneyland, Abby checked out some colleges. I had no idea that a person could get a degree without setting foot on a campus."

Abby nodded. "I knew about earning undergrad degrees that way, but I've been surprised at all the options for the graduate level—even PhDs, and from highly regarded programs. I need something that will let me stay at the ranch as much as possible."

She looked over at Jess and the twins, her eyes filled with so much love that it made Chloe's own heart ache. Those relationships were all still so new, yet in Abby's expression Chloe could see such depth of caring, such commitment to a solid future. The twins might have had a rough beginning, but now they were so blessed.

What would it be like to have parents who cherished you and put you first in their lives—even some of the time? She would never know.

She shook off her thoughts and tried to focus on the conversation.

"…so I researched my options for a distance-learning degree months ago," Abby continued. "And I've already applied to the three I liked best. But it really helped to talk face-to-face with counselors and some graduate faculty during our trip. Now I know for sure which one I prefer."

"That's wonderful, Abby." Chloe eyed the breakfast

casserole, made a rough calculation of the carbohydrate content and put a scoop on her plate. "So, you'll be able to finish it all online?"

"Mostly—plus some week-long seminars on campus during the school year. One of them is actually coming up in May."

"When will you know about your acceptance?"

"Any day. And since the program allows a flexible structure instead of strict semesters, I could possibly get registered in time for that seminar. I hope."

"We also looked at some stallion prospects while we were in California." Betty looked at Jess. "I thought they were all beautiful, but you're a lot more discerning than I am. Have you made a decision?"

He lifted another caramel roll from the pan in front of him and put it on his plate. "Probably the sorrel in Sacramento, if we can agree on a price."

Abby gave the twins a pointed glance, then looked at Chloe and shook her head slightly, clearly wanting to avoid any conversation involving the visit with the girls' mother.

"So," she said brightly, deftly changing the topic. "I would love to hear about what you've been doing since leaving here. You were what—around eleven?"

Chloe shifted uneasily in her chair and took a slow sip of coffee as she sorted through what she could share and what was better left unsaid.

"Nothing much to tell, really. Dad and I moved on to his next ranch job. My mom suddenly showed up and took me to live with her in Omaha, then later we moved to Minnesota. I finished grad school at the end of fall semester. A pretty ordinary life, really."

Abby leaned forward, her interest piqued. "What was your major?"

"A bachelor's in English, and an MFA in creative writing."

"Wow. That's wonderful. I've heard that some of those programs involve finishing a publishable book of some kind as a final thesis project. Did you have to do that?"

"Publishable and actually *being* published are two different things, but yes. I finished mine, though by the time I was halfway through, I'd realized that adult literary fiction wasn't what I wanted to pursue. I started to change my focus to young-adult fiction, but then… well, things changed. I lost my job when the company went under."

Betty stirred some sugar into her coffee. "When you called about coming to Montana, you mentioned a job in Kansas City. You didn't sound very happy about it, though. Have you found something else?"

All of the adults were now looking at Chloe, their expressions curious. They would be even more so if she told them why she'd left the Twin Cities. But that wasn't going to happen.

She cleared her throat. "No, I haven't looked. I'll work for my sister and brother-in-law for a year or so, then reconsider. But I'll still be working on my writing during my free hours, so it's all good."

Though *good* was a relative term. Her father's tarnished past would pale in comparison to what had happened to her in Minneapolis, even if it had been entirely unfair. But once she had a good reference on her resume, for a reasonable amount of employment, she could start over somewhere else.

At the other end of the table, she saw Devlin looking at her, his brow furrowed. A little chill crawled down her spine.

She could tell that he was thinking too hard about what she'd just said. Maybe guessing that there was much more to the story. What if he googled her name? Would he believe the newspaper articles, or would he believe her?

She looked down at her plate and started to pray.

Chapter Thirteen

Friday dawned clear and bright, with the promise of a beautiful day ahead. A day to get a lot done, Chloe promised herself as she settled in front of her laptop on the breakfast bar and got to work.

The twins had gone back to school this morning, so there were no sounds of children playing and dogs barking floating up the trail; no little visitors around to appear at her door with hopeful expressions and hands outstretched for a cookie or two.

But now, with perfect solitude in the middle of thousands of acres of cattle range and government land, where the only sounds were horses whinnying, cattle bawling and bird calls echoing through the pines, she couldn't concentrate.

She'd been bouncing back and forth between the internet news and the Word document she was supposed to be working on.

And it was all Devlin's fault. Not that he knew it.

Since the rest of the family had returned home, she couldn't stop thinking about the strangely wistful expression on his heart-stoppingly handsome face during breakfast on Thursday morning, when he'd reassured

Bella that her milk spill had been perfectly okay. Then later, when he'd playfully teased the twins about renaming their vagabond pony Rascal, and their puppy The Bulldozer, and told them about the pony's daring escape.

When he was with them, it was almost as if all of the darkness in his life peeled away, revealing a glimpse of the man he might have been if not for his cruel father. His sister's death. Going to war.

Was he thinking about the kids he'd never had? His future and the family he could have had with Gina? She wouldn't pry. It wasn't her business. But he'd almost seemed melancholy, and that touched her heart.

He must have been through so much in the military, and then during his recovery afterwards. He certainly deserved happiness now.

Lost in thought, she didn't register the knock on her screen door until she caught sight of someone—a dark silhouette—looming in the doorway.

Panic seized her heart as she launched off the barstool and sent it flying, barely catching herself with the edge of the counter. A stack of papers fluttered to the floor.

"Oh, my word—I'm so sorry," Abby exclaimed through the screen door. "I didn't mean to scare you. Are you all right?"

Shaken, with her heart still thundering against her ribs, Chloe straightened, her hand still tightened in a death grip on the edge of the counter. "You must think I'm crazy. Sorry—please come in."

Abby came inside and rested a hand on Chloe's arm. "Can I make you a cup of coffee?"

"There's fresh coffee in the pot and I've got a warm blueberry coffee cake on the counter, if you'd like some."

Abby served herself some coffee cake and poured a cup of coffee, then stood at the counter and took a bite. "Mmm. I'm quickly learning to never, ever turn down anything from your kitchen, Chloe." She savored another bite. "Have you thought of opening a bakery?"

Chloe managed a small smile. "No, but thanks for the thought."

Abby looked up from her blueberry coffee cake. "My goodness, girl. You are seriously pale. Are you all right?" Her eyes widened. "You didn't…um…have any trouble with Devlin while we were gone, did you? If he scared you in any way—"

Startled, Chloe raised her hands palm out and shook her head. "No. Not at all."

Abby still looked dubious. "I'd never met him until he showed up at ranch Sunday before last. But Jess said he was pretty wild when he was younger, and he still seems to have quite a…well, an attitude. Half the time he won't even answer me."

Chloe bit back a sharp retort. *Poor Devlin. How often was he completely misunderstood like this?*

"He won't want to admit it to you, but in addition to his visible scars, he's deaf on the right side and impaired on the left. He seems to hear deeper male voices better. And his right eye has some permanent damage, as well," Chloe said. "You need to talk louder and be sure he can read your lips, and then he does pretty well."

Abby frowned. "Couldn't he have some sort of surgery? Or use hearing aids?"

"That's what I thought. But his hearing isn't good even *with* his hearing aids. They don't seem to help that much, and apparently his hearing is likely to fade altogether over time."

"Oh. That poor, poor man," Abby said faintly. "I didn't realize."

"I didn't either, at first. I thought he was being arrogant and ignoring me. Once I realized the truth, I practically had to force him to admit it. Then I started badgering him about finding newer and better procedures, better hearing aids, or even letting me work with him on American Sign Language. But...well, he hasn't been very receptive. Yet."

"You know how to sign? I've always wished I knew how."

"I know a little, and apparently Dev learned some while at the VA hospital. But he's resistant to learning more, which is very shortsighted if you ask me. But there are lots of great videos on YouTube, so I've started studying up on it anyway. If he won't work with me, at least I can give him a list of good links."

"What a great idea." Abby seemed to be regarding her with new respect.

"You know, I'll just be here for a few months, but he'll be your brother-in-law forever. It might be a good idea for you to start learning, too. We could even practice together, if you'd like."

"Absolutely!" Abby's gaze settled on Chloe's laptop, and she started toward the door. "But I'd better leave and let you get back to work. I've taken too much of your time already."

"Abby—just one thing. You asked if I had any trouble with Devlin while all of you were gone, and I just want to make sure I was clear. He was a perfect gentleman. And in fact he saved my life."

Abby smiled. "Well, that's good. Sounds like you got along well, then."

"No, not so well. Yet he really did save my life. I

might not be alive if not for him. That's why I was so jumpy when you arrived. An unexpected sound, suddenly seeing someone I wasn't expecting—it terrifies me all over again. I want you to know that he's a real hero in civilian life, not just as an ex-Marine."

Abby's mouth dropped open. "What on earth happened?"

Chloe reiterated her encounter with the Dooley brothers.

"They're back in prison because of their parole violations, and they'll go to trial for this latest crime. But just the thought of them scares me still," she admitted. "I've had some nightmares."

"I'm so sorry." Abby shuddered. "I don't blame you a bit."

"I did nothing to encourage their attention. It was completely random. Yet… I keep feeling like I could have avoided the whole situation. Like I should have *done* something."

"But you did. You disabled one with pepper spray and avoided capture by the other one. I think you were incredibly brave. I can't even imagine how terrifying it was."

"Not brave. Scared…and so relieved when I saw Devlin coming. Has anything like that ever happened to you?"

Abby bit her lower lip. "The closest I ever came was last year, when a hired hand made a crude pass toward me and wouldn't take 'no' for an answer. Remember when I mentioned Grandma Betty and her rifle? She held him at bay, and then Jess and a deputy showed up almost right away. It wasn't nearly as frightening as what you experienced, yet I had nightmares about what might have happened if Betty hadn't been there. But it does get better—I can promise you that."

Devlin rode Trouble up to Chloe's kitchen window on Saturday morning and knocked lightly on the frame. "Hey, Chloe, can you come outside for a minute? I have something for you. Jess's orders."

Through the window he could see her sitting at her laptop, frowning at the screen, her fingers drumming on the breakfast bar. She startled and straightened abruptly, turned to the window, then visibly relaxed.

"What do you need?" she asked as she pushed the screen door open. Her eyes widened when he urged his buckskin forward and held up the reins of a second horse he'd saddled and led up the trail. "Who's this?"

"Bart. Jess figures both you and his horse need to get away from the home place for a while and enjoy some fresh air."

"Really," she said dryly. "His horse needs fresh air? I think I've seen that one out in the pasture. Every single day."

"New vistas, then. Jess is rotating a herd of cattle into one of the Cavanaugh pastures tomorrow, so I'm going up to ride the fence. Want to leave that computer for a while and ride along?"

"Hmm. Sit in the cabin or go riding? Hard decision."

"It's three hundred acres of pretty country, and you won't go hungry." He patted his offside saddlebag. "Betty insisted on sending enough lunch for six cowhands."

"And coffee?"

"She covered that, too."

She grinned up at him. "Give me five minutes."

She was outside in three, wearing jeans, boots and a

faded maroon University of Minnesota sweatshirt. With her ponytail pulled through the back of her black baseball cap, she looked so young and happy that he was glad he'd listened to Jess and saddled an extra horse.

They rode at an easy clip down the gravel road in companionable silence, the warm April sun and crisp mountain air feeling like a gentle balm to his soul. Here, the world of the Middle East, all of that tension and danger, seemed like it was a million miles away.

Chloe turned her head toward him with an expectant look, and he wondered if he'd missed hearing her say something over the steady clip-clop of the horses' hooves.

"I didn't realize how much I've missed this," she said, raising her voice. "Thanks for inviting me to come along."

"Until Jess came back, I was mostly tied down with chores and training the two-year-olds in the arena. I'm glad to be out here." He gave Trouble a pat on the neck. "I think this ride outdoors will do this colt good, too."

"He's sure nice. Is he an outside training horse or one of the Langfords'?"

"Langford bred. He'll be going to a sale in Denver the end of May, though if I was going to stick around, I just might want to keep him."

"So you aren't going to stay here?" She glanced at him in surprise. "I thought after you were here a while…"

He shook his head. "Montana holds few good memories for me, as you probably know."

"But with your dad gone…"

"I won't ever move back here for good." He stopped his horse, dismounted and opened a wire gate along the side of the road.

Once he closed the gate behind them and remounted, they started riding along the four-strand barbwire fence to check for rotting posts and downed wires.

The deeply rolling pasture, with its lush, early spring grass and backdrop of the snowy Rockies, belied his words. The grandeur of it all made his heart ache for what he'd missed all these years, here in the shadows of God's most beautiful creation. And all he would miss in the future.

He dismounted, lifted a section of sagging barbwire and hammered it to a wooden post with a U-shaped fence staple, then tackled the strand of wire below it.

After he finished the section of fence, they rode on to the top of the next rise, where a vista of ranchland spread out beneath them. To the west, the house and barns of the ranch were partly hidden by a heavy stand of pines, and beyond were sawtooth peaks of the Rockies on the horizon.

"This is a beautiful place, isn't it? Just like a postcard." Chloe twisted in her saddle to look at him. "So, what happened to the Cavanaughs? They were nice folks, as I remember."

"Foreclosure. Dad kept a close eye on this county and swooped in to snap up property whenever he could."

"But if he hadn't nabbed it, then someone else would have, right? I can see why he'd want to buy adjoining land if he could."

"You were probably too young to understand what Dad was capable of, when you lived here. There's good reason why a lot of folks around here resent anything to do with the Langford name."

"So, what did he do?"

"The Cavanaughs were struggling that year, like a lot of other ranchers because of drought. Dad basically had the bank in his pocket, and he pulled some strings to make sure they weren't offered any leniency when they fell behind on their mortgage. When they went under, the foreclosure auction was poorly advertised and he bought this place for pennies on the dollar. They were good folks, Chloe. And he treated them like dirt."

"That's so sad. He could be a cruel, hard man toward his family and people who worked for him." She propped an elbow on her saddle horn and rested her chin on her upraised palm as she admired the beautiful landscape. "I remember kicking him in the knee when I was seven, because he'd been mean to my dad."

Devlin laughed out loud at the memory. "I saw that and thought it was the best thing ever because no one ever crossed my dad. My brothers and I wouldn't have dared."

"Maybe it was a little too impetuous, though. He tore into my dad about me being a brat, saying we'd need to leave if I ever did that again. I got grounded in our cabin for three days."

She studied the view toward the mountains. "So, did he buy up any other ranches adjoining yours?"

"The Nelson place, but that was years ago. He got the Branson ranch through a foreclosure sale just before he got sick."

"So, what did he do with all of that land?"

Devlin shrugged. "It all got absorbed into the home ranch—part of the pasture rotation for livestock. He sectioned off the buildings and twenty acres or so from each ranch for rental."

"He was…quite a business man," Chloe said tactfully.

Devlin reined his horse toward the fence line again and Chloe followed. "Dad always told people that he wanted to fend off wealthy buyers from the West Coast who were trying to gobble up property for their vacation homes and resorts, so he could keep this part of the Rockies pristine." Devlin snorted. "Such an honorable goal. But the truth was that he only wanted to build his empire—and have each of his kids take over a surrounding ranch. But Heather died young, and none of us boys wanted to come back."

"Except Jess."

"Not him, either. He dreamed of following the rodeo circuit to save money toward vet school. He wanted to share a vet clinic with one of our cousins. But he was the good son, who gave up his dreams to come back and take over the ranch when Dad got Parkinson's and started to fail." Devlin tried to rein in the bitter edge in his voice. "I'm not proud of the fact that Tate and I found excuses to stay away."

"But you were in the midst of your military career. You couldn't just come home."

"I could've tried for a hardship or dependency discharge, though. I *should* have. But Dad and I were always like oil and water, and he didn't want me here, but I should have been here for Jess."

He hadn't ever admitted it aloud, but it was true.

Chloe stared at him, aghast. "Your dad didn't *want* you here? What kind of man treats a son like that?"

"The day I left for the service, he said that if I chose the military over my family duty at the ranch, he didn't want me coming back. I was to never set foot on the ranch again. And it wasn't just a fit of temper—he meant every word. To make it even more clear, he said he planned to disinherit me."

"Oh, Dev. I'm so sorry." She stared at him, her face a mask of shock and horror. "That was so unfair."

"My choice wasn't part of his plans for the future of the ranch, and no one defied my father." He shrugged away her concern as if the past didn't really matter. As if he no longer cared. He hoped she believed it.

"Being Dad, he never relented. And after he got sick, I figured it wouldn't be good for him to have me around to aggravate him when he was already in such fragile health. But I still should have come back to help Jess, and just kept out of Dad's way, somehow. Even now I regret that I didn't. I failed Jess, the ranch and even my dad when they needed me most."

"You've got that wrong." Chloe's eyes sparked with indignation. "Your dad was the least forgiving man I ever met, and he failed *you* from the time you were a boy. I wish I could tell him about the harm he did. How much he hurt people. He had no right."

Dev could imagine Chloe standing up to him right now, toe to toe and refusing to back down, just as she had as a little girl, defending her father. The image almost made him smile.

"The irony is that after he passed away, the lawyers discovered his will had never been changed…so maybe he'd just bellowed a threat in a fit of anger."

"Yet he never asked you to come home."

"No. And I figured I had my military career, so if he didn't want me in his life, so be it. I didn't need his money or his ranch. What I wanted was to have my father back, but I guess we were both too stubborn and too proud…and then it was too late."

She sidestepped Bart closer to Devlin's horse and reached over to rest a hand on his. "I'm so sorry, Devlin. Truly. That's just so sad."

The touch of her small hand on his warmed his heart and made him wish they were standing on their own two feet instead of on horseback, so he could pull her into a comforting embrace.

"Dad did teach me one last thing I won't forget." Devlin looked over his shoulder to the east, toward the Langford ranch. "No matter how bad things are, you've just got to try harder. Because you can't ever make peace with the past after someone is gone."

Chapter Fourteen

Walking into the Pine Bend Community Church on Easter morning, surrounded by the Langfords, brought back so many memories that Chloe's heart felt like it was overflowing. How many times had she walked through these heavy oak doors with Grandma Betty and the three boys?

Pastor Bob was still here, greeting folks at the door. He was as portly and jovial as ever, though his hair had silvered and he didn't remember her at all.

"Chloe Kenner," she repeated. "My dad was a foreman at the Langford Ranch for a few years, but he didn't come to church. I always came with Betty and the Langford boys."

Recognition sparked in his warm brown eyes. "Now I remember. You were a sweet little thing—with such beautiful red hair. My wife always said she wished we'd had a daughter just like you."

Chloe thought for a moment. "Five boys, right?"

He chuckled. "Good memory. But now we have our girls—five daughters-in-laws whom we dearly love. It happened in God's good time and we just had to be patient."

The sweet scent of the Easter lilies and the burning candles at the altar filled the air as Chloe followed the rest of the family through the narthex, where church members were quietly chatting, and on into the sanctuary.

Jess, Abby and Betty filed into a pew near the back, with the twins alternating between them, and Chloe followed. They were not only on time, she thought with a smile, but the girls had avoided all potential mud puddles and other disasters, and were adorable in their matching pink ruffled Easter dresses, white patent shoes and little white purses.

Chloe twisted in her seat and looked toward the back of the church. Dev had received a phone call just before leaving and had promised to follow in his own vehicle. But where was he? He'd certainly looked grim when he'd walked away with his cell phone at his ear.

She gazed up at the twelve towering stained glass windows depicting Bible stories—six on each side of the sanctuary—that had entranced her as a child. Sunshine beamed through the windows on the east side, sending rays of brilliant color slanting across the pews.

"It's wonderful to be here again," she whispered to Betty. "It's such a beautiful old church. Just sitting here gives me such a sense of peace."

"I've been coming here since I was a baby. I know just what you mean." Betty reached over to give her hand a quick squeeze and nodded toward a couple sitting a few pews away. "Have you met Abby's dad and new stepmother? Don and Darla Peterson are the nicest folks. They'll be coming for Easter dinner."

The organist began to play "Beautiful Savior" just as Devlin slipped into the end of the pew next to Chloe.

"Sorry," he said in a low voice. "After the phone call, I saw someone I knew out in the narthex and I couldn't get away."

The family had filled the pew and there wasn't much room left. Even when Betty scooted over a few inches to make room, he was so close that his leg brushed against Chloe's skirt. She could feel the warmth of him and breathe in his faint scent of pine-and-sandalwood aftershave.

He'd carried her to his car after the Dooleys had tried to assault her along the highway. He'd held her after she'd become woozy outside her cabin.

But this was the only time she'd been this close to him without being in the midst of some sort of an emergency, she thought wryly. And by the time the service was over, she couldn't focus on anything but him—this masculine, kind, wounded protector from her past.

It was staggering to think of all he'd been through as the son of a heartless man. An injured warrior. A man who had lost a woman who must have been the love of his life, since he'd refused to even talk about her. And yet he was so sweet and kind to Jess's little girls, and had been thoughtful in so many ways. He'd even bared his soul to her about his nightmares, though she knew he'd hated to reveal that weakness to anyone.

Her heart melted a little more with every day she saw him at the ranch, even though she knew there was no point in thinking beyond these few months.

Her sister had offered her an incredibly generous job opportunity in Kansas City so that she could claw her way out of debt. An opportunity she could not afford to refuse.

And Devlin would move on as well, to find happiness and fulfillment far away from the ranch that held so many bad memories.

But she would always wonder about what might have been.

After church, everyone headed back to the ranch, where the kitchen instantly became a flurry of activity with Abby, Betty, Darla and Chloe tackling Easter dinner.

Abby's father, Don, played a board game with the twins in the living room, to keep them from being underfoot in the kitchen, and Jess went out to the barn to check on a mare that had foaled during the early morning hours.

After looking in on the new filly with him, Devlin headed up to his cabin to change from his sport jacket and slacks into jeans and a navy oxford shirt, and let Daisy outside for a while.

Much more adept at managing her cast now that it had been almost two weeks since her surgery, Daisy hobbled around to do her business and whined when Devlin put her back in the cabin.

"Sorry," he murmured, cradling her neck between his hands and ruffling her fur. "It's too far for you to walk to the house, and there's too much commotion today anyway. Maybe next time."

At the purr of a motor coming up the trail, he turned and saw Chloe pull the four-wheeler to a stop. She'd changed as well, from a pretty blue skirt, sweater and heels, into jeans and a deep green sweater that made her complexion glow and seemed to spark the ruby highlights in her hair.

"I figured you'd come up here," she called out to him. "How is Daisy doing?"

"I let her outside, but she really doesn't want to be left alone again. She's almost like Velcro, wanting to stay by my side wherever I go."

"Why don't you bring her down? She can hitch a ride in the four-wheeler. When I said I was coming up to my cabin to change, Abby told me to drive up and see if you wanted to bring her."

"I figured there was just too big of a crowd."

"Nah. The twins love her, and she's really sweet and quiet. No trouble at all. That's a direct quote from Jess." Chloe grinned. "It's Poofy who's the problem. He thinks the house is his racetrack and has been ricocheting off the walls since we got home. I hear he'll be banished to the yard when we eat."

"Then there's something to be said about peaceful middle age. Right, Daisy?" he said as he lifted her into the back of the four-wheeler and climbed into the front, next to Chloe. "Thanks. I always feel guilty about leaving her alone."

"When does she go back to the vet for her checkup?"

"The appointment was Thursday, but I moved it up to tomorrow. I just want to make sure she's healing well, but she'll probably have her cast on all of this month and maybe a few weeks into May."

"I hope they weigh her. She looks so much better already, and even her coat is starting to grow back. Can I come along? I'd love to hear what the vet has to say."

He hesitated, "If you don't mind a couple other errands on the way. I need to pick up some things for Betty, unless someone else goes to town sooner, and I want to stop at the sheriff's office."

"To see your old friend?"

"If Lance is there." There it was again—the same flicker of emotion he'd seen in her eyes when the deputy had come to arrest the Dooleys out on the highway and she'd realized who he was. "Otherwise I just need to drop something off for him. I get the feeling you don't care for him much."

She cut a quick, troubled glance at Devlin as she pulled to a stop in front of the house. "Both of you were five years older than me, so we were basically on different planets. I didn't know him."

A tactful nonanswer if he ever heard one, but apparently she wasn't going to elaborate.

Once they were back in the house, Chloe disappeared into the kitchen to help with the final Easter dinner preparations, while Daisy headed for her favorite spot by the fireplace and kept a watchful eye on the twins until Betty called everyone to the dining room.

Jess laughed when Daisy followed the girls to the dining room table and sat dutifully behind their chairs. "Look at that. She thinks she's guarding her little herd of sheep," he said. "She wants to keep them safe."

Chloe faltered to a stop, a platter of sliced ham in her hands. "I hadn't thought of that. What if she wasn't Farley's service dog? What if some rancher had her guarding a herd of livestock and she got hurt, then wandered off? He could want her back."

She looked so stricken that Devlin lifted the platter from her hands and put it on the table. "You said you posted notices all over town, though. Someone would've seen them by now and passed the word. Right?"

"Or they might in the future." Chloe bit her lower lip. "I know that's what these dogs were bred for, but I'd feel bad if someone picked her up only to drop her off in the middle of nowhere, with a flock of sheep."

After Grandma Betty led the family with table grace,

the adults began passing an array of serving dishes that didn't seem to end.

Even Sunday meals offered a plentiful variety of foods, but this—his first family holiday meal in almost ten years—blew Devlin completely away.

Ham. Tender roast beef. Mashed potatoes, au gratin potatoes and bowl after bowl of different vegetables. A half dozen salads and Grandma Betty's homemade cloverleaf rolls that were so buttery and tender that they melted in his mouth.

By the time the dishes were cleared, he couldn't imagine eating another bite. But then, after the first round of dishes were in the dishwasher, the desserts were set out on the oak buffet in the dining room.

Bella's awestruck eyes rounded as she walked along the buffet and looked at the towering cake with lemon-curd filling, topped with fluffy frosting dazzled with pastel sprinkles on top. And three kinds of pie.

"I want a taste of *everything*," she said.

Abby steered her back to her chair. "Let's start with the one you think you'll like best, sweetie, and go from there."

"Thanks, Abby, Darla and Chloe. Having all of this help has been quite a change from when the boys were young and I was the only one doing the cooking." Betty brought in a fresh pot of coffee and began refilling cups. "Back then I did as much as I could beforehand, but by the time everyone was served I just wanted to go lie down."

"I can only imagine," Chloe murmured as she began serving the desserts as everyone asked for the one they preferred.

Betty stopped behind Darla and rested a hand on her shoulder. "At Christmas we were all truly blessed to welcome Don and Darla to our Christmas dinner, and Abby, of course. Now I can't envision a holiday meal without them."

From across the table, Devlin saw tears shimmer in Darla's eyes as she quietly reached over to hold her husband's hand.

"Thank you, Betty—and everyone," Darla said, her voice wavering. "You probably can't imagine what this means to me. And Don, too. If my daughter wasn't with her dad this weekend, I know she would've loved to be here, as well."

Darla had to be a good twenty years younger than Don, if not more, and her platinum hair, heavy makeup and flashy sequined shirt were definitely a contrast to her ranch-weathered husband. But the look of love that passed between them was unmistakable.

For all of their differences, they had something he would never have, Dev realized, feeling a twinge in his chest. He wondered if they knew just how blessed they were to have been able to make a good life together.

Things didn't always turn out that way.

At church he'd been so acutely aware of Chloe sitting next to him that he'd had trouble focusing on the first hymn, though when Pastor Bob began his message he'd sat up a little straighter when the man's gaze seemed to land on him for a moment before moving on.

The Easter message had been about Christ's death and resurrection, and the forgiveness of sins that offered life everlasting to those who believed.

After the pastor spoke of the power of prayer in asking for forgiveness, he'd said that since Christ grants us grace and forgiveness, so too we must have the courage and strength to forgive each other *and ourselves*. And to continue to condemn ourselves for past mistakes was to deny the power of that forgiveness.

How many times had he heard this message while sitting next to his brothers under the watchful eye of Grandma Betty? Yet this time the pastor's rich, mellow voice seemed to strike home in a deeper way.

Forgiveness.

But was that even possible after all the ways he'd failed those he loved and the guilt that still consumed him?

After all the times he'd prayed so hard for something, and his prayers hadn't been answered, he'd begun to doubt God even listened to him. His prayers hadn't saved Heather or Mom or Gina. They'd all died anyway.

Yet Betty had never doubted, never questioned, he was sure of it. She held on to her faith like it was a beacon of hope that would never dim.

Maybe someday, if he tried harder, he could have a faith like hers.

Dr. Wendel beckoned Devlin and Chloe back into the exam room, where Daisy was lying on a stainless steel table, with the older vet tech at her side.

"I looked at her new X-rays, compared to the first set, and Daisy has done remarkably well for a dog that was so debilitated when she came in. The bone realignment is still in position and she's healing as expected."

At the sheer delight on Chloe's face, Devlin smiled. "What about the cast?"

"I think it can come off in about five weeks or so, if her X-rays still look good."

"Dev has been really careful about limiting her activity." Chloe stroked Daisy's head. "How is her weight?"

"Up almost eight pounds, which is excellent progress." The vet scanned the information in Daisy's chart on her iPad. "Since we had no old records on her, we had to start from scratch. Last time, we gave her a first rabies, plus all of the vaccinations she needed as an adult dog. Do you have any questions?"

Develin and Chloe exchanged glances. "I don't think so," he said. "At least not right now."

"Have you had any responses to your posters about finding her?"

Chloe shook her head. "Nope. But when my cell rings, I keep hoping it isn't someone wanting her back."

"Well, one thing you might try is asking some older folks in town if they knew Leonard Farley or know someone else who might have," Dr. Wendel mused. "Maybe one of them could help you identify the dog as his and put your minds at ease. I have an older client right after you who might be able to help. I think she has lived in the area for years."

Out in the waiting room, a silver-haired woman sat with some sort of fluffy dog in her lap. When Chloe and Devlin came out, she wrapped her arms around her little dog and gave Daisy a wary look.

"What a sweet little dog you have," Chloe said. "By any chance would you have known Leonard Farley or know someone who might have? He had a cabin up in the mountains and died a few years ago."

The woman shook her head, still keeping a firm grip on her dog. "No idea. You could ask at the post office, or maybe the bank."

At the bank, no one had heard of him. At the post office, the single clerk behind the counter appeared to be in her twenties and had never heard his name, either.

Chloe sighed as they stepped back out onto the sidewalk and headed for Devlin's SUV. "At least it was worth a shot—"

The color drained from her face and her steps faltered, her eyes riveted on the Minnesota license plate of a white sedan. She scanned both sides of the vehicle. Then her gaze swept the sidewalks on both sides of Main Street.

"Who are you looking for?" Mystified, Devlin looked at the car, then back at her. "Is something wrong?"

"No. No—not at all."

Which was totally implausible, given her sudden level of tension.

"You're sure?"

With a quick shake of her head, she strode to the side of his SUV and climbed in as soon as he hit the lock button on his key fob.

There had to be a lot of other things he didn't know about her, even though they'd known each other long ago, he realized as he helped Daisy into the back of the SUV. Anything could have happened during the intervening years.

And there was yet another question that had been simmering at the back of his mind since the day she'd arrived. Sure, she'd had a plausible explanation.

But really, who would drive a thousand miles from Minneapolis just to hole up in a little cabin for months to write when there could've been hundreds of other options closer to home?

He turned to face her after he got behind the wheel and started the engine. "Seriously, you look like you've seen a ghost. Is everything all right?"

The worry in her eyes and that faint glimmer of a smile didn't look very convincing. "I... I just saw a

Minnesota plate on a car that looked like one an old friend had. But I'm sure it wasn't the same car."

Right. The appearance of an "old friend" wouldn't send her into a state of shock.

And come to think of it, what was the *real* reason she'd seemed so wary of Lance? Because he was with the sheriff's department? Yet the thought of Chloe ever having more than a parking ticket on her record was beyond imagination.

He pulled out of his parking spot and headed down a few blocks to Miller's Amish Market and Café. "Betty wanted me to pick up some things for her in here. Do you want to come in?"

She shook her head. "It does look really interesting, but I'll go when I have a lot more time to browse. I'll just stay here with Daisy."

"Really?" He took another look at the large plate glass windows of the storefront, which were filled with stacks of colorful quilts, knitting yarn and all sorts of gifty-looking handcrafted doodads that had to be appealing to the local women and any tourists passing through. What woman would not be eager to go in there?

Someone who didn't want to accidently meet up with someone from her past, maybe, if Chloe's reaction to that white car was any clue.

After picking up Betty's yarn, he drove on to the sheriff's office, where he pulled to a stop once again. He looked over at Chloe and draped one hand over the wheel. "Is there anything you want to tell me?"

She tucked a swath of her auburn hair behind her ear and fixed her gaze on a woman pushing a baby stroller down the sidewalk. "Not really. I'll just wait out here if you're going in."

"Are you in some kind of trouble?"

Startled, she shot a glance at him. "Goodness, no."

"If you need help of any kind, you just need to say so."

"I don't. Everything is fine, really." But she didn't meet his eyes.

Chapter Fifteen

This is for you, Grandma Lydia, Chloe whispered as she collected a stack of spiral notebooks filled with notes on her recipe experiments, opened up her laptop and fired it up.

Rain drizzled down the windows, obscuring the beautiful view in every direction, making it a perfect day to work inside her cozy cabin, with a small, cheery fire crackling in the fireplace.

She took a sip of cherry tea and contemplated the stack of empty boxes she'd brought out of the closets last night. She'd been on the verge of packing, but then stopped.

The white car with Minnesota plates had startled her yesterday. Reminded her of just how vulnerable she still was.

Even with the care she'd taken when she'd left Minneapolis, someone with good sleuthing skills could probably find her anywhere. And what then? She hoped she could count the people here as friends who would believe her.

She'd done nothing wrong. Her expensive lawyers had represented her well. But a smarmy supermarket-tabloid reporter had all but driven her out of town anyway, with his lies and innuendos, and if he followed her here, he might follow her to Kansas City too, and then what?

Holly had been kind to offer her a good job, but even she couldn't be expected to accept having her company's name dragged through the mud just to help out her sister.

At the sound of a gentle knock, she spun around and peered through the little peephole in the door, then flung the door open. "Abby! My goodness. Come in!"

"Sorry about the mess," Abby said as she toed off her high rubber boots and hung her raincoat on the coatrack by the door, then dropped two shopping bags on the kitchen counter. "I just had to show you something—oh."

Her eyes widened as she turned and took in the pile of boxes in the middle of the floor. "You aren't leaving, are you? Please say you aren't."

"No." Chloe knew she would need to explain sooner or later, but hopefully not just yet. "I'm…uh…going to break down those boxes so they'll lay flat and slide under the bed. They're taking up too much room."

"Okay. If you say so." Abby gave her a searching look. "I haven't seen either you or Devlin around since Sunday, so I thought I'd come up and see if you're all right. I hoped the two of you hadn't had a big falling-out or something."

"That's a little hard when you aren't exactly an item in the first place," Chloe said with a laugh. "I'm just here working, and since Jess is back to doing at least most of the chores, Devlin might be working on remodeling that cabin he's in."

Abby's brow furrowed. "Not an item, you say. Really?"

"He's not looking, and neither am I, which is perfect. We can just be friends for the time that I'm here, with no awkward complications."

"Hmm."

"It's true."

"So, tell me—why isn't he looking?'"

"I gather that he had a girlfriend who passed away. I don't know the circumstances or when, but I'm guessing that she must have been the love of his life, because he refuses to talk about her. Poor man."

"Okay, I can buy that. Unless it's been like a decade ago, and then it's just an excuse to not even try. But what about you—why aren't you pursuing this opportunity? You're lovely, smart and obviously talented—you could help him move on, right?"

Chloe thought back over the romantic failures she'd been through. The last one, which had been by far the worst of all. Words failed her, and all she could do was shake her head.

"Personally, I think you two are perfect together. So does Betty, and she knows the two of you better than I do."

Chloe drew in a pained breath as it all came back to her. Her phone call to the ranch in late March, inquiring about any rental cabins during April. Betty's exuberant response—and her pure innocence when she said that the only brother at the ranch was Jess.

If Betty hadn't known about Devlin's plans by March, she'd certainly have known about his arrival days before Chloe had arrived. And she hadn't said a word.

"That stinker," Chloe exclaimed. "She *knew*."

"Knew what?"

"And no doubt she was trying to be a matchmaker.

Which is unbelievably optimistic, given that Devlin despised me when I was little. Which, by the way, Betty knew. She constantly scolded him about being nicer, and it never helped a bit."

A small smile tugged at the corner of Abby's mouth. "Apparently you haven't noticed the way he looks at you, then."

"Like I'm an alien, probably. That was one of his nicknames for me when I was ten. I think I graduated to Froggy when I was eleven."

"Actually, his gaze sort of follows you when you walk by, and it's more of an 'I can't believe she's this beautiful now' look. And don't be offended, but I see the way you look at him, too. And there is *definitely* something there, whether you want to admit it or not. It took me way too long to learn this lesson, but some things are far too precious to waste."

Chloe laughed. "You are going to be a wonderful mother to those twins. You're already quite the storyteller. Bedtime will always be an adventure."

"I hope so. The longer I'm here, the more I love them. I can't even believe how much. And Jess—he's already the most wonderful daddy." Abby seemed to glow with happiness from within, but then she grew somber. "When I think about what they went through when they were younger, it's all I can do not to cry."

They both fell silent for a moment, and then Abby reach out for Chloe's hand. "But I didn't come here to be all teary-eyed, really. I came bearing gifts—some yummy leftovers from our big dinner yesterday—and I also wanted to ask your advice. Have you ever planned a shotgun wedding?"

Chloe stared at her. "A what?"

"Sorry." Abby flapped a hand against her mouth

and chuckled. "I meant a short-notice wedding—like in June."

"I haven't, but I'd be glad to help...as long as I'm still here."

"It probably seems impulsive, since I just came back to the ranch last fall. But it isn't, really," Abby said earnestly, as she dumped one of the bags out onto the counter. She'd brought some bridal magazines and a ream of printouts from online bridal sites. "Jess and I dated through high school and college, and back then we'd assumed we would eventually get married. But we had a fight, broke up...and here we are, all these years later, finally getting things right."

"A happily-ever-after, after all."

"Exactly. And I really regret wasting all of those wonderful years." A twinkle sparkled in Abby's eyes as she gave Chloe a measuring look. "Something to think about, because time marches on, and you can never get it back."

She made it sound so simple. An easy decision, and then you could have a happily-ever-after, too.

But Dev was clearly bound by deep wounds from the past and grief over a loved one. And she had learned the hard way that love didn't last, trusting someone with your heart was a dangerous thing and one inadvertent mistake could lead to notoriety that never, ever went away.

Devlin pried off the last damp strip of wallpaper covered with garish pink and green salmon and stuffed it into a black plastic trash bag.

He could not imagine his mother or grandma ever choosing something this awful for the bathroom of a cabin. The wife of a long-ago ranch hand maybe?

Whoever it was, they'd used industrial-strength wall-paper paste, or maybe even household glue, and they'd even plastered the paper all over the ceiling. He'd been soaking and scraping it for two days, during spare moments between other projects, until his bad shoulder ached and his neck muscles were in knots.

Even with the paper finally off, thick swirls of petrified wallpaper paste still adhered to much of the wall surface.

He filled a plastic spray bottle with warm water and vinegar and sprayed a section of the drywall, then began wiping it off a section he'd sprayed several minutes earlier.

"How about you do this for a while and let me watch?" he called out to Daisy.

She thumped her tail in happy acknowledgment, her large dark eyes never straying from him.

He'd ordered a therapeutic memory-foam dog bed for her online, and she'd dragged it from the bedroom into the living area so she could rest in perfect comfort, while keeping a watchful eye on him throughout the whole process.

As nonchalant as he'd been at the vet appointment on Monday, he agreed with Chloe.

Maybe Daisy would love doing what she'd been bred for, but the thought of this sweet dog spending the rest of her life out in the elements, watching a flock of sheep, instead of staying at his side, made him hope that she would never be reclaimed by someone else.

Chloe.

He hadn't seen her since Monday, but he hadn't stopped thinking about her, either.

Betty had sent up enough Easter leftovers to last him until tomorrow, so he'd stayed at his cabin ever since coming home from the vet clinic. He'd been working on a long list of the renovations he needed to complete before starting on the next cabin, though at this rate it might take until next Christmas.

Maybe there'd been a perfectly good reason for Chloe's reaction to that white car in town, just as she'd said. Maybe she didn't care much for Lance because he'd teased her when he'd come to the ranch as a teenager. As Devlin recalled, the guy certainly hadn't been very nice to his siblings, so that was possible.

Assuming the worst—that she'd wanted to avoid a deputy because she was in trouble of some kind—must have been insulting, to say the least.

He studied his progress and sighed. One small corner of one wall done, with more than three more walls to go.

"What do you think, Daisy—do I owe Chloe an apology?"

"I'm not sure why, but if you need to ask, then I'd say definitely yes."

Startled, he spun around and found Abby grinning at him from the bathroom doorway. "I didn't hear you knock."

"Sorry. I did, but then figured you couldn't hear me. Your grandma wanted me to drop off some of her chocolate chip cookies on my way to meet the girls at the bus stop." Her brow furrowed as she brought her hands up and awkwardly signed *How's it going?*

He felt a flush work up his neck. "You don't need to do that."

She lifted a shoulder in a slight shrug. "Chloe has been helping me, and it doesn't hurt to learn. I certainly want to be able to talk to my future brother-in-law, whatever the future brings."

So Chloe had been telling everyone about his disabilities? They might eventually figure it out on their own, but admitting to it still felt too personal, like revealing a weakness that he didn't want to share.

He pointedly turned away and began wiping off another section of glue.

"Denial won't get you anywhere, Dev. You might as well let her help you before she leaves. I actually think it's a pretty cool skill. And in case you didn't know, your hearing loss isn't a secret you can keep," she added gently. "Anyone who speaks to you for a while will probably figure it out."

He froze. "She's leaving?"

"She says no, but when I saw her yesterday she had a pile of boxes on the living room floor. And that looked mighty suspicious to me."

Chapter Sixteen

Chloe stretched her arms above her head, then slumped back in her chair.

She'd been working for hours today on the first draft of her young-adult novel, and since coming to Montana she had reached page forty. But now it seemed as if she was deleting five words out of every ten she wrote, and even then she wasn't satisfied. Why weren't the words coming easier?

It wasn't hard to guess.

Since going to town with Devlin on Monday, she'd been edgy and uncertain about what to tell him...or not. But what was the point, really?

It wasn't like she and Devlin were an "item." And it wasn't like she was hiding a terrible truth.

But just the thought of revealing her naiveté and downright stupidity was embarrassing to say the least. And those awful headlines...

If Devlin happened to google her name, find them and start asking questions, she would certainly speak up. If not, maybe she could just let sleeping dogs lie, and slip quietly off to Kansas City with her pride intact.

"Hey, Chloe—got a minute?"

Surprised at the sound of his voice outside her door, she looked down at her ratty gray sweatshirt and worn jeans, and tried to remember if she'd even brushed her hair this morning. Probably not.

"Just a minute," she called out. On her way to the door, she took the long way to glance in the bathroom mirror. "This is pathetic even for you," she muttered to herself.

She made a quick change into a decent sweater, pulled her hair back into a low, sleek knot at her nape and went to the door.

He stood on the outside step, holding a plastic bag filled with homemade cookies. "Grandma sent way too many. I thought I should share."

Just seeing him always sent a little shiver of awareness through her, though now her first impulse was to accept them, say thanks and politely say goodbye. He'd been suspicious about her reaction to that white car in town, and he'd asked if she was in trouble. What if he asked more questions? She didn't want to lie. She wasn't even good at it. But the less she had to talk about the past, the better. And maybe the less time she spent with him, the better it would be, as well.

She'd once thought her childhood infatuation with him was just that—a silly figment of her imagination, a preteen's first, innocent crush. But apparently it had never gone away. And since coming back to the ranch, it had only grown stronger.

She knew he had to be self-conscious about his scars, but they no longer even registered when she saw him. He was still the tall, dark and lethally handsome guy he'd always been, and with every day she stayed at the ranch she felt even more attracted to him, and even more vulnerable when he was around.

He was looking at her expectantly, and she belatedly realized that she hadn't answered; she'd just been staring. "Um...thanks. Would you like to come in?"

He glanced down at his worn clothes and gave her a self-deprecating smile. "Maybe for just a minute. I've been working on my cabin and there's a lot more to do."

"So, what have you been up to? Wait—let me guess." She looked up at a little flutter of paper on his shirt, then moved a little closer. "Wallpaper? With...*fish*?"

"Salmon. Great big salmon. With an occasional bear in the mix."

She shook her head, laughing as she took the cookies and set the bag on the kitchen counter. "I've got a herd of enormous elk in this bathroom—probably dating back to the sixties. Someone must have gotten a great deal on wallpaper that was destined to never sell."

"My dad would've been impressed with the price, if nothing else. From what I can see in my cabin, he didn't spend a nickel on keeping anything up." He glanced at the interior of her cabin, with his gaze lingering on the living area. "I understand this cabin was Jess's doing. Before the last ranch hand was hired, he did do some updates."

He was just so easy to talk to that she didn't want him to leave. "Coffee?"

He hesitated, then shook his head. "I suppose I should be going. Is everything going all right?"

"I asked Betty for a list of some names of her older friends, and she gave me twenty phone numbers, so I've been calling to see if any of them remember Leonard Farley. I talked to some and had to leave quite a few messages for the others, but so far I've been able to cross off fifteen names. No one remembers Leonard, much less whether or not he owned a dog."

"It's almost like the man never existed." Devlin frowned. "I can ask Lance next Monday night, when we meet for pizza at Red's. Maybe he can look up the investigation into the discovery of the body. If there's any mention of Daisy, we won't need to worry about someone trying to claim the dog."

"Good." She managed a stiff smile. "Thanks for stopping."

She ushered Devlin outside, then closed the door and leaned against it. *Pizza, with an old pal from his wild teens.*

Right.

She'd forgotten about Red's until she passed it on Main Street a few days ago, and then she'd remembered it all too well. The weathered exterior, forever in need of a coat of paint. The neon beer signs in every window. The faded sign reading Burgers and Pizza on the front door. And the fact that her dad had hung out there way too often.

Lance had been the wildest of Devlin's high school bunch, never absent when a group of Devlin's buddies showed up to party out in the woods. She'd seen him stagger to someone's car and barely get into it before collapsing across the seat. Devlin had been no better. And now they were hanging out together again like old pals.

Chloe tensed as more old memories flooded through her thoughts.

It had always been innocent, necessary little trips to town with her dad. Quick "cups of coffee" with an old pal. An errand. But though he could saunter back to their cabin as if he hadn't touched a drop, he'd invariably returned with bloodshot eyes and liquor on his breath. And then the fights had started—with Mom livid, and Dad angry and self-righteous. And Chloe would end up hiding amongst the dust bunnies under her bed, praying her parents would forget she was there. Even the smell of alcohol was still enough to make her ill.

She'd tried to block all of those memories and instead remember an idyllic childhood in Montana, with caring parents who had always put her first.

But maybe it was good that she'd just been jerked out of her fantasy.

Devlin was a handsome charmer, sure enough, and she already knew it would be way too easy to fall for him. Maybe she already had.

But he and his buddy were probably still the same. And if so, then letting herself care too much for someone like her dad would be a terrible mistake.

Chloe had always been the sweetest little thing. So earnest, so helpful. Always wanting to defend anyone she loved from every possible foe.

That young version of Chloe had grown up into a complicated woman he just couldn't figure out.

She'd been hesitant and even a little rattled when he'd come to her door, though he couldn't imagine why—unless it had something to do with her odd, wary behavior in town. He'd begun to wonder if someone might be stalking her, when she'd turned so deathly pale at the sight of that car.

Yet when she finally welcomed him into her cabin a few minutes ago, she'd been friendly and they'd even laughed over the wild wallpaper in their cabins. But then, like turning a faucet from warm to cold, she'd practically booted him out the door.

He'd had a chance to glance around her cabin,

though—his main reason for stopping by—and he'd seen no evidence of moving boxes anywhere, so maybe she'd told Abby the truth about planning to flatten all of those boxes for compact storage. At least that was reassuring.

The alternative—the possibility of her abruptly disappearing in the dead of night—sounded erratic and even dangerous. If she was uneasy about something, wouldn't she be safest here among people who knew her and on an isolated ranch where no stranger could appear unnoticed?

Tomorrow he was going back to her cabin and they were going to have a good long talk.

Back at his cabin, he let Daisy out for a short walk, then brought her inside and started back on the petrified swirls of wallpaper paste that coated the bathroom walls.

A message alert chimed on his cell phone.

It was Jess. Someone had called the ranch number wanting to speak to him, and they'd left a number with an unfamiliar area code that might have been in the New York City area, though he wasn't sure. Strange. Someone selling insurance or pushing investment opportunities?

He ignored it and went back to work. But when Jess texted again and said the guy had called once more, Devlin relented and prepared to tell him to get lost.

The guy answered on the first ring. "So, tell me, cowboy—were you in on the scheme from the beginning?"

At the guy's nasal twang and insinuating tone, Devlin pulled the phone from his ear and hit the end key. Scheme? What kind of sales call would start like that?

The caller instantly called back. "I've got your number now, so you might as well talk to me. I can keep hitting Redial all day long."

Devlin gritted his teeth and reached for the power button to turn the phone off, but the man kept talking.

"How long have you known Chloe? Did you know about her being complicit in that big financial-services scandal in Minneapolis? Were you up in the Twin Cities during the trial? Did you know she faced serious jail time until her boyfriend let her skate away, free as a—"

Devlin drew in a harsh breath. "I have nothing to say to you."

"Then maybe you should listen—though you might not like what you hear."

The guy sounded as smarmy as they came: sly and crafty, with a wheedling edge to his voice that made Devlin's skin crawl. But he couldn't bring himself to disconnect the call and turn off his phone just yet. Was this why Chloe seemed so nervous in town when she saw the Minnesota license plate? What on earth was she mixed up in?

"How did you get my number?"

"Easily, cowboy. I just saw you and her in town, and asked around. Everyone around here seems to know the Langfords. And hey, with GPS I even know where you all live. I want some time with that girlfriend of yours. I need her side of the story by tomorrow night, or I can just make something up. Your call."

"So you're a reporter, then."

"You might say. I don't always worry about the facts as much as some. What sells the most copy is the stuff I write. Flamboyant stuff, you know—like pretty young things who get involved with rich guys, looking for a cozy life, then try to take the poor guy for a ride. Like your Chloe, for instance."

If even a fraction of this were true, what did that mean for her? Had she gone on the run? Was she wanted by the police? Devlin reached for a pen and the back of an envelope and started jotting notes. "I have to say that it sounds like you've done your homework. Who did you say you write for?"

The guy named a cheesy tabloid Devlin had seen in several states, then rattled off a series of accusations that made his blood run cold.

"I'll tell you what." Devlin lowered his voice to a growl. "You might not ever hear from her, but now I've got your number, too. And if you bother her again, I can promise that you'll *definitely* be hearing from me."

Chloe had just dropped a bag of trash into the receptacle outside when she saw Devlin striding down the trail. From the grim set of his jaw, she guessed he'd either had bad news or he was delivering it. When he stopped in front of her, his eyes blazing, she knew which it was. She hadn't been mistaken about the car, the license plate or what was to come, and the thought of it made her sick.

"We need to talk."

"Fine," she said heavily. "Come on in."

She led him inside and started a pot of coffee, then settled at the round oak kitchen table.

He sat down across from her and studied her so intently for a moment that she wondered if he could read her deepest thoughts. "Just out of curiosity, why are you moving all the way to Kansas City for a job you don't seem to want?"

She drew in a long breath. "Money. Time…and security, I suppose."

"I don't suppose you can elaborate."

"I had just enough cash to cover my stay here—three months to follow my dreams, before taking a job with my sister's company. It will pay very well and help me clear my debts. While staying with her and her husband, I'll feel more secure. And it will give me time to get back on my feet. Hopefully without drawing unwanted attention."

He sat still, quietly waiting for her to continue.

"I suppose you're here because you've met Wylie. I have to apologize for that. I never thought he'd follow me here, but I guess his name really does fit."

He locked his gaze on hers. "I'm guessing that less than 10 percent of what he says is true. Do you want to tell me your side of this?"

"Will it even matter?"

"Try me."

"People tend to believe what's on the TV news and in the newspapers, and I'd guess my name is pretty much destroyed by now—at least in the Minneapolis area. In fact I know it is. Even with my credentials, I wasn't able to find a new job after I was released." She gave Devlin a weary look. For all his pretense of fairness, she knew he'd probably already made up his mind about her. She could see it in his eyes. "But the reporters like Wylie can smell blood a mile away, and he's been harassing me ever since. He likes the angle of a pretty young charlatan taking advantage of a rich, married, middle-aged man, I guess. I wanted to leave town and get as far away as I could, and this ranch seemed perfect. The cabin rent was inexpensive, and I thought he might give up looking for me. Then I could go on to Kansas City. The last thing I want is for Wylie to stir up bad publicity for my sister's company because of me."

"So, what happened to get you arrested?"

"I worked for a privately owned investment-management company while putting myself through my undergrad and graduate-school degrees. Thad was my boss. He gave me good raises, praised my work. He flirted a lot and after a while, we started dating. It seemed perfect at first. He took me to fine restaurants, the theater, romantic walks out at the Arboretum, sailing on the St. Croix river. He promised me the moon—saying we were going to have a wonderful life together, and I was gullible enough to believe him."

"I'm guessing this didn't end well."

Embarrassed, she shook her head. "All the while, he was embezzling heavily from the company and laying a complicated trail of evidence that led directly to me. He ended up siphoning off over $800,000. I had no idea until his whole scheme came crashing down. The owner became suspicious and hired a team of forensic accountants who came in at night, and then one day I got arrested. Thad totally threw me under the bus. He blathered on about how I had been scheming to use him as a cover for my crimes by claiming to love him—how I'd tried to manipulate him into leaving a wife I didn't even know he had. It just got worse and worse as he fed lurid details to the reporters, who hung on his every word. I was headline news for a while—even in the major newspapers."

"But you're free now."

"Thanks to my lawyers. I was finally exonerated, but now I'm nearly broke. I took out every loan I could get and maxed out my credit cards, and I still owe them money. But I'll pay off every dime if it's the last thing I do. Without them I'd be behind bars for something I didn't do." She gave a bitter sigh. "I still can't believe

I was so utterly naïve. Why did I fall for someone like that? Why didn't I realize I was being used? After all that drama, I'm pretty sure I'll never trust another man again."

Chapter Seventeen

On Monday evening Chloe finished up her third batch of Grandma Lydia's Swedish meatballs of the day, ladled it into a stainless steel bowl and put it in the refrigerator. Tomorrow she would lug all three batches down to the house at suppertime and ask everyone to do a taste test, comparing them all.

The second batch was likely the winner, she guessed, but she wanted to be sure before adding the final version to her cookbook.

With original directions, including ingredients like "one package of ground beef, plus one of fresh ground pork," with no weight or fat percentage listed, and a portion of butter "the size of a pullet's egg," there was plenty of room for guesswork, and she wanted to make sure every recipe was perfect.

"So, where is your buddy, Daisy?" she asked. Devlin hadn't been sure what time he'd get back from town, so he'd brought Daisy and her dog bed to Chloe's on his way down to his SUV.

Daisy had been curled up on it ever since, her dark eyes following Chloe's every move.

She glanced at the time, then pressed her lips together and started cleaning up the kitchen. It was already past ten o'clock, and Dev had said he was meeting Lance after his day shift ended at six. How long did it take to eat a pizza at Red's? Unless the place had changed radically, it was known more for its bar than the food, and they'd always served frozen pizza heated in their oven. There was never much of a wait.

But Chloe couldn't imagine those two spending a whole evening choking down pizza that tasted of cardboard and freezer burn.

In their bad-boy days in high school, they would have been downing beers behind the barn, with Lance ending up too drunk to walk. She shuddered, imagining the two of them driving their vehicles home with innocent, unsuspecting drivers on the highway. Families in minivans, heading up into the mountains for vacation. Truck drivers looking forward to getting home after a long haul. She looked at her cell phone lying on the table. Should she call and offer them rides home? Would they be embarrassed or grateful? Were they already driving home?

She finally sent Devlin a quick text. Then she second-guessed her decision as she dusted and swept. Daisy suddenly sat up and stared at the windows, her ears pricked and tail wagging.

"Is he back?" Chloe asked her.

The dog whined and went to paw at the door.

Chloe turned on the outside light and looked through the screen door, expecting to see Devlin coming up her path to pick up Daisy. Instead she could see Lance with his arm around Devlin's waist as the two of them staggered past, heading up to Devlin's cabin.

She stared after them in disbelief. "Lance—is everything all right?" she called out.

Lance, apparently bearing much of Devlin's dead weight, faltered to an awkward stop and shot a look at her over his shoulder. "Had too much," he wheezed. "He'll just sleep it off."

Her heart plummeted. For all that she'd known of Devlin's rowdy high school years, since arriving at the ranch she hadn't seen a single bit of evidence that he drank anymore. Not even once.

But apparently neither of them had changed, she realized, if Devlin couldn't make it up to his cabin alone and even Lance looked unsteady on his feet. Horrified, she slammed the door and locked it, then leaned against it with her eyes closed. She'd experienced this scenario too many times to count with her father, and now bitter disappointment welled up in her chest.

She'd been falling in love with Devlin, a little more with every day. But Lance had admitted it out loud— Devlin hadn't changed at all.

Devlin hadn't come for Daisy at eight the next morning, or at nine. At ten o'clock, Chloe gave up. "Sorry, sweetie. I'd love to have you all day, but I need to go to town."

She snapped a leash on the dog's collar and headed up the hill to Dev's cabin, half expecting to find Devlin and Lance sprawled against tree trunks along the way, still in a drunken stupor.

But no one was out there—just the squirrels and chipmunks scurrying about, and the birds singing up in the trees. Devlin's door was open.

"Typical," she huffed, her irritation and disappointment rising. "So, so responsible."

She knocked on the screen door, then banged on it

louder. "Devlin! Are you in there? I'm bringing Daisy back. I need to go to town."

The cabin remained silent.

She glanced around the area outside, thinking he might be working on some project, then stepped back and looked up at the roof. He wasn't there, either.

Then she knocked on the door once again. "Devlin, are you in there? I'm bringing Daisy in."

Daisy romped in and headed straight for the sofa. The curtains were all closed, and only then did Chloe notice Devlin was sitting there in the darkened room, hunched over his folded arms. He was still as stone and didn't so much as twitch a muscle at her approach.

Protecting a hangover headache, no doubt. A flashback hit her—of one time after another when she'd found her dad in this same state. Month after month, year after year. Job after job after job. Her dad's love affair with the bottle had ruined the lives of him and everyone around him. Was this the truest side of Devlin—one she hadn't yet seen?

"Devlin—did you hear me? I've brought Daisy back, so you'll need to look after her. When I get back from town, I'll come up and check on her to make sure you did. Okay?"

"Okay." His voice was so raspy and low that she barely heard him.

She didn't try to muffle the closing of the screen door when she left.

Three hours later Chloe had brought her groceries into her cabin, put everything away and headed up the trail to check on Devlin and Daisy. He'd probably be at his kitchen table by now, nursing a cup of black coffee and regretting the day he'd been born, if her experience with Dad was any guide, though no amount of misery ever seemed to stop the cycle from repeating all over again.

Daisy would definitely need to get outside by now, poor girl.

Chloe knocked and then opened the door. Daisy came barreling through, eager to sniff the yard and do her business. *So, I was right*, Chloe muttered as she let the dog back in and stepped inside.

But Devlin wasn't at the kitchen table; he was still on the sofa, though now he had propped an elbow on his thigh and was resting his forehead in his upraised palm.

"Not much progress, soldier," she said, pushing back the curtains to let the sunshine stream in. He groaned the moment the bright light hit the side of his face. "It's already one thirty. You and your buddy must have had one exceptionally good—or bad—night at Red's. You were both staggering when he brought you home. Can I make you some coffee? Toast? Bring you some juice?"

He didn't answer, though she had the distinct impression that he wanted her to disappear. Well, so be it.

"I'll go now, and I think I'd better take Daisy with me until you're back on your feet." She snapped the leash on Daisy's collar and headed for the door. "I hope you'll feel better soon."

She did wish him well—truly she did.

But she now knew one undeniable truth and was deeply grateful for the lesson. One night didn't prove Devlin was out of control, but to her, one was all it took. Her greatest fear had always been that she might end up with someone like Dad, who had managed to hide his problem for so long. And she would never dare trust Devlin again.

Chapter Eighteen

By three o'clock Devlin was able to sit a bit more up-right; the crushing pain on the left side of his head was still throbbing, but without the searing agony of a railroad spike jammed through his temple.

By five o'clock the pain had dimmed a little more and now he felt utterly exhausted.

He blearily scanned the room, trying to remember. Had Chloe been here? Lance? And where was Daisy?

He rose slowly, carefully, trying not to jar his head back into a renewed jungle beat of pain, and shuffled through the cabin. Daisy was gone, so Chloe must have taken her…or maybe she'd never brought her up here in the first place? The last ten hours were a blur.

Someone knocked on the door.

And there they were. Daisy, wagging her tail joyously. Chloe, her mouth pinched in a firm line, with an overall expression somber.

"I see you're back on your feet again, so I thought you might like to have Daisy back," Chloe said. She unsnapped the leash, nodded to him and turned for the door without even a trace of her usual smile. "I'll see you later."

He hadn't heard her clearly, but he could see she was angry. "Wait."

She turned back partway, her eyes stony. "You remember my dad. The alcoholic. Alcohol *terrifies* me. I know its power. And you know full well that it got my dad fired from this ranch."

He nodded, not quite following her line of thought.

"I'll just go ahead and admit it—I've been falling in love with you, Devlin. I thought… I thought you had changed from when you and your high school friends thought it was so cool to get drunk." Her voice took on a bitter edge. "But you haven't. You couldn't even make it up the trail by yourself last night."

He furrowed his brow, trying to sort through all of those words with a head that was still aching. "No. Just…a headache." Though calling one of his severe cluster headaches "just a headache" was like saying a candle was as strong as the sun. Not even close.

She gave him a look of frank disbelief, and then turned on her heel and left.

It was just as well.

His headache had hit with the force of a bulldozer just before he and Lance had ordered pizza. He could show her the proof—the paperwork from the ER last night, where Lance had taken him instead of eating at Red's, and the record of the pain meds he'd received by IV, though they hadn't even begun to touch his pain.

But if she *truly* cared for him, she would believe in him, and she wouldn't need that proof.

The two of them were each probably better off alone.

On her way back to her cabin, Chloe felt the vibration of her phone in her pocket and lifted it to look at the screen. The number wasn't familiar and she usually let unknown callers roll into voice mail, but it was a local area code, and on a whim she answered.

"Hey, Chloe? This is Lance. Dev gave me your number last night while we were waiting in the ER, in case they kept him overnight."

"You two were at the *ER*?"

"Yeah. They released him after the IV meds, but personally I thought he should have stayed overnight. I've never seen anyone in such excruciating pain from a headache. How is he doing today?"

A headache?

She took a deep, steadying breath, already horrified at her mistake. "Last night—I saw you two on the trail when you helped him get home. You said he'd had too much to drink and that he'd sleep it off."

"*Drink?* Hardly. He had a severe headache, plus too much IV pain medication, in my opinion. He was really out of it—but he refused to stay at the ER any longer. He insisted on going home."

She sagged against a tree beside the trail. *Please, Lord, forgive me. And let Devlin forgive me, too.* "Will it come back?"

"Apparently he's had problems for a long time. He'll be fine, and then he'll hit a streak where he gets his headaches at the same time every day. While I was waiting in the ER, I googled the topic, and a number of sites say these cluster headaches can cause the most severe pain known to man. After seeing Devlin, I can believe it. So take good care of him, okay?"

She winced. "Thanks for being such a good friend, Lance. You were wonderful to stay with him and help him get home."

Lance chuckled. "I'm just glad we made it. He's a

lot taller than I am, and that trail to his cabin is steep. I almost lost him once or twice."

After Lance ended the call, she flopped on her sofa and leaned her head against the back, feeling utterly mortified.

Why had she let her own issues cloud her judgment and compassion so completely that she'd failed to realize that Devlin was in pain? Why did she often assume the worst?

That one didn't take much thought.

She assumed the worst because she expected it for herself. She couldn't even guess at just how many ways her family life had affected her...and held her back even now.

No one is the villain in their own story, she remembered hearing in one of her writing classes. She'd liked the concept so much that she'd googled the quote and found it attributed to a dozen sources.

Had Dad, despite his drinking, figured he was still doing the best he could? Had he changed?

Taking out her phone, she tapped the contacts button and scrolled down until she found Dad's number. Her finger trembled over the call button. Would this still be the right number? Would he even answer? She couldn't even remember the last time she'd talked to him, though he'd probably been drunk at the time and wouldn't remember it, anyway.

But maybe it was time to finally get some answers and make things right.

She resolutely tapped the number. Got a disconnected-number recording—no surprise there—then texted Mom. She texted right back with a different area code and number.

This is all I have—but it's a year old, and probably dis-
connected, too. Sorry.

Chloe said a little prayer under her breath as she
made the call and listened to the ring.

Whether or not she was able to make connections
with Dad, she had some apologizing to do...if Devlin
would even let her in the door.

The next day Chloe stepped out of her car in the
ranching town of Keller, Idaho, and surveyed the three-
block length of Main Street. Two dusty pickups were
parked in front of a small grocery, and just one in front
of Patsy's Café—but it was a gleaming black Ford F350
with a ranch logo on the side. Definitely not Dad's.

She'd been on the road since five in the morning to
get to this tiny Idaho town by one o'clock, but was he
even going to show up? After her eight hours on the
road, she sure hoped so.

Dad had made no effort to stay in contact with his
family, and the estrangement had only deepened over
time. Apparently he still moved erratically from one
ranch-hand job to the next, so he had no consistent,
personal address, and he hadn't kept a consistent cell
phone number over the years, either—probably because
he couldn't remember to pay the bills.

She shouldered her purse and stepped into the cafe,
hoping he hadn't forgotten to come. There were a lot of
things he'd forgotten over the years—recitals, elementary school plays, eighth-grade graduation—always
with the excuse that he'd been "busy." But she'd known
better. His "busy" had always been his next bottle, and
she'd always come in at second place.

A tall man in neatly pressed jeans and a faded denim

shirt slowly stood up next to a table in the back and ducked his head in welcome. He held the brim of his Western hat in both hands. "Chloe?"

"Dad?" She blinked, taking in the changes in his appearance. He usually had a grizzled three- or four-day beard, overlong hair and sallow skin. The dirt ground into the cracks and crevices of his hands never washed away, and there'd always been the stain of cigarettes on the fingers of his right hand. He'd always seemed decades older than his years.

But today she saw none of that. This version of her father stood taller, straighter. He'd clearly had his hair freshly cut and instead of being covered in stubble, his face was smooth and tanned. It was oddly touching that he'd made this effort.

"Dad," she said, giving him an awkward handshake. "It's been a while."

He nodded, and now she saw the deep regret—perhaps even sorrow—in his eyes. "That it has. How have you been?"

She shrugged. "Good, I guess. And you?"

They settled across from each other at the table, with coffees that neither of them touched. The awkward conversation between them felt like that of total strangers, and she felt the time with him ebbing away. Urgency spurred her on.

"Actually, I'm not so good. I'm feeling hurt and angry, and I need some answers, Dad. But that's crazy, because being hurt and angry over the past isn't going to change anything at all."

She was babbling, but he nodded as if he knew what she was trying to say. "It hurt, when Mom suddenly came back and took me away from you. No explanation—she just showed up. I thought you loved me, and I felt like a sack of trash being tossed from one place to the next."

"I'm sorry, Chloe. I know I made a mess of your life." He waited, nodding slightly, encouraging her to go on.

She took a deep breath. "It's hard to believe in other people or even yourself when no one has ever cared. I've never been able to forgive you for that. Though I know I ought to—which makes me feel worse."

"You'll never know how much I've prayed for forgiveness for the life you had growing up."

She stilled, not believing the words she was hearing. This was the man who'd refused to set foot in church when she was young. Except maybe at Christmas.

"And I've prayed over all of the mistakes I made," he continued. His shoulders slumped, as if he was wearing a mantle of iron. "I know the good Lord has forgiven me, and I've been trying to be a better person ever since I asked Him into my life. But I won't ask for your forgiveness, because I know your wounds run deep. And for that I'm more sorry than you will ever know."

There were some good memories, too, she suddenly recalled. Dad putting her up on a pony and teaching her to ride. Stopping in town for an ice cream cone at the drugstore. Him singing some silly cowboy song to her when she was afraid of the dark.

"I never saw what real family was like, after growing up in an orphanage. Me and your momma were too young when you were born, sugar," he continued. "Seventeen. We weren't ready, and never really got the hang of being married or having a kid. I'd say we failed in every way. We surely didn't deserve to have such a fine little girl."

She felt tears burning in her eyes, but she blinked them away.

He smiled a little, the fan of wrinkles at the corners of his eyes deepening at some long-ago memory. "You were just the sweetest little thing. Always were. But I was a drunk and I couldn't do right by you."

"You cared more for your booze than you ever did for me," Chloe whispered.

"I have no excuses, sugar. I was the one who called your momma and told her to come get you, because you deserved a better life. You were so angry when she came for you that you wouldn't say goodbye. But I know it was the right thing. Just look at you now, so grown-up and pretty, knowing how to dress and act right. And she made sure you got a good education, too."

Mom hadn't ever been forthcoming about her past, and she'd never been a warm-cookies-and-cocoa kind of mother, but now Chloe began to see her struggles in a different light. Beneath the crotchety exterior, she'd been a single mom who had soldiered on the best she could.

Chloe cradled her coffee cup in both hands and swirled the steamy brew. "I get scared, Dad—I'll think I've found someone good, the right person for me, but then I get spooked because I'm so afraid that he'll... he'll..."

"End up a drunk like your old man."

The harsh, true words bit deep. She felt warmth rise up her cheeks. "You could hide it so well, and that scares me, too. I might not know the truth about someone until it's too late."

He studied his gnarled hands for a long moment before looking up at her. "Just take your time. Don't rush. And whatever you do, pray hard and listen to your heart." He pressed his right hand to his chest. "You'll know here, when it's right. But then you have to *work* at it. The best things don't come cheap."

"Have *you* followed your heart?"

"Never found anyone who could replace your momma. But I found the right place to be, finally. I'm working for a good man of faith, who got me into AA and gives me the encouragement I need every single day. I've been dry for a year and it pains me to look back at all of the years I lost. But now life is good. And," he added with a little smile, "because of him and his wife, I don't miss a Sunday at church. With the good Lord and a lot of prayer, I'm finally finding my way."

She looked at him anew—seeing as an adult what she hadn't seen as a child.

A man who had been little more than a child himself, with no education and a low-paying job on a ranch, who despite his heavy alcohol addiction, had still stayed in his unplanned marriage with an unplanned child. And he'd struggled to support them until he realized they were better off without him.

He'd had a difficult, sad life, but apparently he'd turned himself around. She had no right to judge him for his weaknesses and poor choices. That was the Lord's business, not hers. And now her job was to forgive.

Feeling as if a dark, oppressive weight had been lifted from her chest, she stood and awkwardly extended her hand. "Thank you for meeting me here. I just… I just needed…"

"I understand, Sissy. I do." His callused hand trembled as he enveloped her hand in his and just held on, as if he didn't want the moment to end.

Sissy. She hadn't heard that nickname since the last time she had seen him—while looking out of the rear window as her mother drove away—and it nudged at her heart.

"Maybe we can meet here again sometime. For coffee?" The words tumbled out of her mouth before she could catch them.

A brief, tentative smile tweaked the corner of his mouth and a suspicious sheen filled his eyes. "I would like that, honey. I'll be here any time you say."

Chloe took a final look at the platter of white-chocolate-and-pecan cookies and cranberry-walnut scones, tweaked the red bow, and knocked on the door of Devlin's cabin. It was silly to feel this self-conscious after knowing him all this time, and yet she did. And embarrassed. And even a little shy.

How many times in life could a person possibly survive making such an utter fool of themselves while managing to deeply insult someone in the process? She'd certainly done that and more, and if Devlin never spoke to her again, she wouldn't be the least bit surprised.

He came to the door in jeans and a fitted black T-shirt that made his chest look even broader and more intimidating than usual. Daisy stood at his side like a sentinel guarding the door.

He gave Chloe a cool look. "Need something?"

"I certainly do. First of all I need to give you these, because I am an abominable person who cannot keep her mouth shut, who needs to learn a lesson about thinking before she speaks, and who needs to give you a heartfelt apology."

His level gaze didn't waver.

"And I need to explain. If…um, you'll let me."

She thought she saw a corner of his mouth twitch ever so slightly. She held the platter up a little higher and pushed it toward him until he accepted it. "You'll be relieved to know that there's no evaluation form for critiquing these. They are simply a gift."

He gave a curt nod. "Good. I had to google half of the baking terms on the last one you gave me."

"I'm really sorry I didn't believe you when you came back with Lance. It scared me when you planned on being with him, because he was at all of your high school parties at the ranch, and he invariably got drunk. I just assumed that you two were going to drink too much and then—" she swallowed hard "—and I was afraid that I'd learn that you'd never really changed. If that was true, it would break my heart."

"I did get your designated-driver text. Thanks." He gave her a faint, self-deprecating grin. "Back in high school I did anything I could to rebel against my dad— and I was stupid. But actually, I couldn't drink now even if I wanted to. Which I don't. I've been on daily meds for years that usually control my cluster headaches. The two don't mix."

She stared up at him with relief and awe...and a good dose of embarrassment at having doubted him. "I admit— I'm probably a *little* paranoid about alcohol. With a dad like mine, I can't help but worry. And when Lance said... well, I misunderstood. I care about you. A lot."

"A *lot*?"

She gave him a light, playful punch on the arm, "Of course I care about you—more than you'll ever know, and I always have. Do you want to hear about my meeting with my dad?"

He blinked at the abrupt change of topic. "Uh... okay."

"I started to think about how much trouble I have with relationships. How I always expect the worst, because I already know things won't work out, and then that's exactly what happens. Just as it always was with my dad. I realized that I had to go see him face-to-face and try to make peace with him. To forgive him, really, instead of just letting my anger and resentment grow."

"And how did that go?"

"I figured I would see him for ten minutes and be done. I thought he would be curt, dismissive—probably even drunk, so I would say what I needed to and then walk away."

A shadow crossed Devlin's expression. Was he thinking of his own difficult father?

"Dad works for a man who got him to attend AA and says he's been sober for a whole year," she continued. "Now he even goes to church. He's changed—I think he really has. He said he was truly sorry about the past. After talking to him, I feel like a dark cloud hovering over me is finally lifting. I told him I feared ending up with a closet alcoholic like he was, and he said, 'Just take your time. Don't rush. And whatever you do, pray hard. You'll know in your heart when it's right.' I never would've imagined my dad talking about prayer."

"So, have you followed your heart?"

"I've been really trying to, because I don't want to risk missing out on the one person who could be the very best thing in my life." She swallowed hard and looked up at Devlin, wondering if he could read her thoughts. Wondering if it would make any difference if he could. "But now I'm not sure there's any hope."

He didn't respond to that, though he did seem to relax as he leaned his good shoulder against the doorframe. "While you were gone, Abby told me that you got some good news. She said to ask you about it."

Chloe felt that familiar, funny little flutter in her

midsection whenever she looked up into his stunning silver-blue eyes. "I got an email from my attorneys before I left for Idaho. Thad's trial was delayed for a number of months, but it's finally over. He was found guilty of embezzlement, as well as defamation and tort of malicious prosecution for falsely implicating me."

"Great news, Chloe."

"It gets better. As part of the victim-restitution ruling, Thad has to pay my legal bills, and an additional award has been made for defamation. So I'm no longer faced with heavy debt."

"And now you can choose whatever future you want," he said slowly, his gaze pinned intently on hers.

"Evidence absolved me of any involvement before I ever came to Montana, but these rulings make it doubly clear that I was a victim, not a criminal. So yes."

"What about the reporters?"

"My attorney has demanded an apology and retraction from the newspaper. He said it probably wouldn't hold much weight, but I shouldn't need to worry about being harassed any longer."

He enveloped her in a congratulatory hug that somehow deepened into a longer embrace. "Finally free?"

"Finally." She savored the warmth of his broad chest and felt suddenly bereft when he stepped back. "And believe it or not, I emailed my manuscripts off to a publisher yesterday. I feel like the future could be unfolding in so many different ways now. I just can't wait to see what happens."

He regarded her somberly. "You deserve only the best, Chloe. Wherever life takes you."

His words sounded like a farewell, and she felt her heart start to fracture.

Her legal debts had been erased, but she still needed

a job and her sister was still expecting her in Kansas City. Would he even care when she left?

She'd thought he would, during these past few wonderful weeks. They'd seemed to grow closer with every passing day, She'd hoped he would ask her to follow him, wherever he was going. But maybe she'd been wrong. The fracture in her heart deepened. "I wish you the same, Devlin. Truly."

"Good things are happening for both of us, I guess." His gaze lifted above her shoulder to the thick stand of pine trees to the west, and the silhouette of the Rockies beyond. "Jess put Tate on a conference call with me yesterday, and the two of them made me a proposition."

"About what?"

"They asked if I was interested in staying in Montana for good. Jess needs help, and I could take over the Cavanaugh spread, or one of the two other adjoining properties."

"That sounds wonderful, Dev. Would Tate come back, as well?"

"Getting him to settle down here would be like trying to rope and hog-tie the wind." Devlin shook his head. "He lives only for a 'next rodeo, next adventure' kind of life."

"Did you give them an answer?"

"Not yet. I've spent the past three months doing everything I could to get back in shape, to physically qualify for a job offer in New York. And now they've offered it to me—more money than I thought possible, with advancement in the next two years. It's a once-in-a-lifetime chance at something big. But they need me right away."

New York was a long, long way from Kansas City. She could already see the future. She'd come to care for Devlin more than ever over these past weeks and thought he felt the same. Every embrace seemed longer. Every kiss, sweeter.

But it was all just temporary, and each of them would now move on to their own new lives. The calls and emails would slow, then stop, and then he would forget her. But he would own a big part of her heart until the day she died.

"That's wonderful, Dev. I'm really proud of you."

His gaze locked on hers. "If you were me, what would you choose?"

He'd asked her opinion as if her response truly mattered, and a small flicker of hope came to life in her heart. But he wasn't asking if his choice would affect their future together, or if she'd be willing to follow him. He'd simply asked her advice.

"You need to follow your heart," she murmured, even as her own heart started to break. She already knew his answer. How could he say no? The job in New York was everything he'd wanted. Perfect for a man with his skills and background.

And it wouldn't be long before he walked out of her life. Forever.

Devlin saddled Trouble and headed out into the foothills to clear his thoughts.

I don't want to risk missing out on the one person who could be the very best thing in my life. But I'm not sure there's any hope.

He'd understood exactly what Chloe was saying when she'd looked up into his eyes. It had been all he could do to just stand there and not sweep her up into his arms. But despite the small ember of hope flickering in his chest, he knew she deserved so much more than someone like him.

As a kid, he'd seen and experienced so much injustice under the thumb of his father, yet it had made him who he was. A warrior, with a strong sense of purpose. A fierce protector. He'd been fiercely protective of his sister and mom, and Gina, too.

But with that had come the crushing guilt and sorrow when he hadn't been able to save them. Not even one.

As a young boy, why hadn't he been there at the right moment to save Heather from the wheels of Dad's truck? To help his mother deal with her sorrow before she died? If he'd spent more time with her, talked to her more, been a better kid, could he have made a difference? Helped close that ragged wound in her life?

Yeah—the coroner had called it a heart attack, but even as a kid he'd always known the truth. She'd never stopped quietly crying at night when she thought no one could hear her. She'd never gotten over Heather's death. Until finally, less than a year later, her broken heart just…stopped.

And he would never, ever stop regretting the day he'd been running late and asked Gina to meet him at a restaurant instead of going to pick her up. If he hadn't selfishly asked her for that small favor, she wouldn't have been in the wrong place at the wrong time for a drunk driver to snuff out her life on a busy highway.

Coming back to the ranch had been a form of penance. A place to lose himself in the day-to-day chores, to partially atone for his failure to come home and help Jess out when Dad was sick. And essentially a place to simply escape the outside world and accept that he would never really be whole.

But now he started thinking about what Chloe had said about her father.

Instead of harboring a lifelong undercurrent of anger and resentment toward him, she'd decided to make peace with him, and to make peace with her own troubled past.

Could he do that, too—accept that the past was over? Maybe that was what he needed to do.

As the words of Pastor Bob's Easter sermon came back to him, he finally understood the undeniable truth.

If God was so willing to completely forgive all of the ways Devlin had failed, then how could he hang on to his own stubborn arrogance and pride? Like Chloe, he needed to finally forgive his father and let the past go.

Chloe. Just her name touched a chord deep in his heart. Did he dare take a chance? She deserved far better than a guy like him, but if he held back, would he risk missing out on the one person who could be the very best thing in his life?

From the top of a knoll overlooking the ranch, he surveyed the vista before him—the ranch buildings, looking as small as a child's play set from this vantage point. And there, to his shock, was Chloe, slamming the trunk of her car and embracing everyone who had come outside to wish her farewell. She was *leaving*?

She had declared her feelings for him, and what had he done? He'd been an absolute fool. How could he let her go? He reached for his cell phone, but it wasn't in his pocket.

From up here he could see the mile-long ranch road, following a sweeping curve around a stand of pines and winding past several deep ravines before reaching the highway.

If he rode cross-country, he just might make it to the pasture fence running along the highway before she did.

He needed to talk to her face-to-face before she disappeared. Reining Trouble toward the highway, he urged him into a lope and started to pray.

Chloe drove slowly down the lane leading to the highway and toward the rest of her life, feeling empty and a little lost. She'd planned to stay longer, but what was the point?

It hadn't really taken long to pack, and the sooner she got to Kansas City, the sooner she could start getting her life in order.

She could start working for her sister's company sooner. During her long, empty evenings, she could work on her writing. But the thought of the coming weeks, months and years without Devlin was already breaking her heart.

She'd just reached the highway when she noticed something moving fast over the gently rolling pastureland, scattering a herd of fat Black Angus cattle. She pulled to a stop and stared as Devlin appeared over the last rise, bent low over his buckskin gelding's neck.

"Chloe!" He pulled to a stop, then swung down from the lathered horse and led him over to meet her at the fence. "I can't let Trouble stand still," he called out ruefully. "Not when he's this hot. Walk with me?"

Trying to suppress a smile, she climbed over the fence to join Devlin as he sauntered with the reins in his hand. "Um…is there something you need?"

He stopped and turned to face her. "I need you. And if I don't make this right, I will regret it for the rest of my life."

She looked up at him and searched his beloved face. "And how are you going to make this right?"

Resting his hands on her shoulders, with his gaze locked on hers, he said, "By telling you that, yes... Yes, I care—more than you'll ever know, and—" Trouble reached out with his nose and knocked Devlin into Chloe, as if impatient to get this over with and get back to the barn.

Laughing, Devlin pulled Chloe into an embrace and then a kiss.

"I was blind for so long," Devlin said, "But I don't want to make that mistake again. Stay here at the ranch—or let me follow you wherever you want to go. But just don't walk away."

Chapter Nineteen

The beautiful June morning had dawned clear and bright, offering the perfect weather for setting up the rows of white wicker chairs in a small clearing on a hill overlooking the house and barns of the Langford ranch.

Just relatives and close friends had been invited for the intimate ceremony, though the caterers from Pine Bend were setting up a casual buffet nearby, to which the entire community had received an open invitation.

Devlin and Tate, dressed in black suits, formed half of the wedding party, while Abby had asked Chloe and Darla to be her attendants.

"This will be truly memorable," Chloe said, leaning close to adjust Abby's pearl necklace. "I'm so thrilled to see this day finally come."

Abby eyed the twins, who had been herded by Betty toward a card table and given colored pencils and paper to keep them busy. "I'm just hoping those flower-girl dresses make it through the ceremony without a major disaster. They begged for a princess style with masses of lilac tulle and sequins, but it won't go well if they bounce up against the needles and sticky sap of these pine trees. And you know Bella…"

"They'll be fine, and if there's a little boo-boo or two, you'll just have something to laugh about later," Darla said. She tugged the jewel neckline of her pink silk sheath into position. "Though I do look forward to seeing how they manage eating some wedding cake."

Chloe laughed. "By then it probably won't matter."

With a last measuring glance at the little girls, Betty walked over to them, her eyes twinkling. "You all look so beautiful."

"And you are stunning, Betty," Abby kissed her wrinkled cheek. "I'm so glad we all opted for individual colors instead of being matchy-matchy. The photographs will be so pretty."

Betty smoothed the skirt of her lacy mint-green dress. "I've dreamed of the day when all three of my grandsons settled down, and it's finally happening. About time, too. I've waited way too long, and I want to live to see my great-grandchildren."

At the confident tone in her voice, Abby and Chloe exchanged glances. Betty *had* played a hand in the way both of them had come to the Langford ranch. Had she been working at subtle matchmaking efforts all along?

"Just one of the boys is getting married, Betty," Chloe pointed out, holding back a grin. "Devlin has never talked about plans, as far as I know. And as for Tate, wedding bells aren't even on his radar. I asked him earlier if he was serious about anyone and he actually cringed at the thought. Cringed!"

Betty looked up at her with a small, secretive smile. "You never know."

Abby watched Betty go back to the twins, then leaned close to Chloe with an upraised eyebrow and an assessing expression. "So, what did *that* mean?" she whispered. "Is there something I should know?"

"Maybe she has her eye on someone for Tate? I can't see how that would help, since he so rarely comes home."

"That wasn't the brother I was thinking about," Abby retorted dryly. "I'm wondering about a certain ex-Marine who keeps glancing this way. You are stunning in that shade of yellow, by the way. It really sets off your auburn hair and beautiful complexion. You are positively glowing."

The photographer beckoned to Abby and motioned her toward a backdrop of pine trees for some photos,

Chloe watched for a while, then looked across the clearing to where the three Langford brothers were deep in conversation, struck by how much they looked alike.

Tate had just flown up from Texas last night, so she hadn't had a chance to say more than hello and a few brief words, but she could see that he definitely had the Langford charm.

Tall, dark and fit, all of them looked like they might have come for a high-end magazine shoot instead of a wedding.

As always, Daisy stood close to Devlin, and for the wedding festivities she wore a big pink satin bow attached to her collar. With her cast off, her coat grown out to fluffy white splendor and her quiet, majestic countenance, she looked as if she was a dignified member of the wedding party.

Devlin broke away from the group and sauntered over to Chloe, kissed her cheek, and led her off to one side.

"You're beautiful, as always," he said, brushing a kiss against her other cheek. "I'm so glad Abby and Jess have such a perfect day for this."

Tate gave an earsplitting whistle and grinned as everyone startled and turned his way. He nodded toward the pastor. "I think it's time to start, folks."

At Pastor Bob's direction, the wedding party and the guests moved into position and the violinist began to play. The sweet, pure notes seemed to lift into the crisp mountain air, and Chloe felt her eyes start to burn. It couldn't be a more beautiful wedding: two people so in love, a wedding day so perfect that she felt a tear of joy trace down her cheek.

Even the two flower girls seemed to be in such awe that they stood perfectly in place, with none of the shenanigans they might have pulled when they were younger.

Chloe felt a little tug at her heart. She might never see these people again, she realized sadly. As much as she enjoyed them, they weren't relatives, and she was just a temporary guest who was renting a cabin. Nothing more.

Since the day she'd almost left early for Kansas City, she and Devlin had spent all of their spare time together. Trail riding, moving cattle and sharing dinners in town, at her cabin or when joining the others at the main house. They'd talked late into the night about a thousand different topics with her hand in his, or his arm slung around her shoulders—mostly in agreement, and sparring playfully over the rest.

But she'd fallen in love with Devlin long ago and thought he felt the same, after what he'd said earlier. Yet since then he'd said nothing more about a happily-ever-future. Even when she finally *asked* to talk about it, he'd shied away.

A classic case of cold feet? So be it.

He would soon go ahead with his plans to leave for New York, and she would be heading for Kansas City.

She had too much pride to ask again…even though she'd soon be leaving behind the people—and one particular man—who would always own a big part of her heart.

After the ceremony, the wedding party and guests joyously congratulated Jess and Abby, then slowly drifted toward the buffet, but Devlin came over to take Chloe's hand and move her away from the crowd. "Did Doris Mason talk to you yet?"

"Who?"

He canted his head toward a stocky woman with silver hair who was talking to the pastor. "Betty asked her about Leonard Farley. Apparently Doris rented a house to him before he moved up into the mountains, and she remembers him getting a new Pyrenees service dog just before he left. She said she'd always thought the dog's black ear was comical, as it reminded her of when her kids were young and got into a can of paint. Apparently they tried to paint their house cat."

"So Daisy became a stray after his death?"

"Exactly. So no more worries about someone else claiming her. She can be ours without question, according to Lance."

"Oh, Dev—that's wonderful!" She blinked, and her heart stumbled. He'd said *ours*.

He grinned down at her. "I was prepared to offer any amount of money to whoever might show up to claim her, but now we don't need to worry."

Daisy, pressed against his thigh, looked up at them both with a big doggy grin, her tongue lolling, as if she knew exactly what they were saying.

Devlin tipped his head toward the edge of the small clearing. "I want to show you something—just a short way up the hill. It's a beautiful view."

He led the way to a breathtaking promontory overlooking the western edge of the Langford Ranch, the neighboring Cavanaugh ranch and the Rockies beyond. "What do you think—does the old Cavanaugh place look like a welcoming home to you?"

"It's beautiful, Dev. Like a dream come true. It's wonderful to think that it could be yours, if you decide to stay."

"I have. I've realized that this is where I belong."

It was the right decision for him. She could hear it in his voice, and she was happy for him…even as the empty place in her heart seemed to expand.

"The other two ranches aren't visible from here," he continued. "But I plan to look at them on horseback. Would you like to come along? It should be a pretty ride."

She'd been so entranced by the view that she hadn't realized that he'd withdrawn something from his pocket.

He held out a small box that looked very old and delicate, with gold filigree tracing its surface and fragile hinges. She drew in a shaky breath, almost afraid to take it. He put the box in the palm of her hand and gently curved her fingers around it.

His eyes locked on hers. He slowly raised his hands. Hesitated. Then he slowly, perfectly signed *It was my mother's. I hope you'll like it.*

She felt her jaw drop.

For several heartbeats it seemed as if the entire universe stood still.

He'd done it. He'd actually *done* it for her. A perfect gift. An acknowledgment of how hard she'd wanted to help him prepare for whatever the future might bring.

"Oh, Dev…" She felt tears burn in her eyes as she reached up to cradle his face against her palm. Then she raised up on her tiptoes to brush a kiss against his lips. "That was awesome! But how—when—"

"YouTube. Just like you said," he said with a self-deprecating smile. "I've been watching videos. I wanted this moment a week ago, but I wasn't ready. So Abby helped me practice."

"But—you'd been so set against it. Why…"

"I guess I always knew the docs were right—that I should prepare for all possibilities. But I was too stubborn to admit it." His smile faded. "Maybe being deaf and damaged seemed like part of my penance for the times I've failed the people I loved."

"You've never failed anyone, Devlin. The bad things that happened to them were *not* your fault."

A rueful smile briefly touched his mouth. "You and Betty have told me that so many times that I've lost count, but I was too stubborn to listen. But now I'm working on accepting it. And I've finally accepted what the future might bring. If there's any way to prevent it, I don't want to live in a silent world. Not if you are part of it." He raised his hands to sign once more. *But if that isn't possible, at least I can be ready.*

She stepped into his embrace and he tucked her head beneath his chin and held her, as if he never wanted to let her go.

"I've also been searching on the internet for clinics and procedures that might be able to help me. I took the first diagnosis as fact, but I've discovered that I don't want to just give up. Not yet." He released her, rested his hands on her upper arms and took a step back. "I believe that's exactly what you said I should do when you first came back to the ranch."

Happiness welled up inside her until it felt as if her

heart could burst. "I'm so happy for you, Dev—I'll do everything I can to help."

"Start by opening that box," he said, with a teasing smile.

She blinked. Fumbled with the tiny hasp, then finally managed to lift the velvet-lined lid.

Inside lay a glittering brilliant-cut blue topaz ring.

She looked at it in wonder, then up at him. "Oh, Dev—it's stunning."

"It matches your eyes so perfectly that I wanted you to have it." He brushed a sweet kiss against her lips. "Will you marry me?"

His gaze locked on hers, and her heart caught in her throat as she looked up at him and saw the future—a lifetime of love with the man she'd fallen for when she was just a girl. Dreams really do come true.

"Yes—a thousand times, yes," she whispered.

"If you'd rather have a diamond…"

"No—this is absolutely beautiful, and because it was your mother's, it means even more to me."

He wrapped his arms around her and kissed her, and her heart overfilled with joy.

* * * * *

If you loved this story,
pick up the first Rocky Mountain Ranch book,
Montana Mistletoe
from top author Roxanne Rustand.

And don't miss these other great books
in her miniseries Aspen Creek Crossroads:

The Single Dad's Redemption
An Aspen Creek Christmas
Falling for the Rancher

Available now from Love Inspired!

Find more great reads at www.LoveInspired.com.

Dear Reader,

Thank you so much for joining me in Montana ranch country.

High Country Homecoming is the second novel in my Rocky Mountain Ranch series, and this book was such fun to write. It combines some of the things in life that I love the most—faith, strong family connections, horses, dogs and country life…and cooking! And it even provided a nice reconnection to a wonderful old friend, attorney William Roemerman, who helped with legal aspects of the heroine's past.

My husband and I live out in the country with three horses, two rescue dogs and a number of rescued kitties. I've had horses since I was a little girl of six, so whenever I start a book series set in ranch country, it makes me feel right at home. And in this book, my heroine Chloe is an avid cook—a woman after my own heart.

Since she's working on a cookbook with recipes gleaned from her beloved grandmother's recipe box, I thought you might like to try one of those recipes—which is actually a recipe that I have been making for decades!

If you enjoyed this book, you can check harlequin.com or other online bookstores for the first in this series, Montana Mistletoe. The third title will be out in early 2020.

You can reach me at: www.roxannerustand.com, http://Facebook.com/roxanne.rustand, http://Facebook.com/roxanne.rustand.author.

Or by regular mail at: PO Box 2550, Cedar Rapids, Iowa 52406

Wishing you a lifetime of blessings,
Roxanne Rustand

Grandma Lydia's Chocolate Chip Cookies

3 sticks (1 ½ cups) salted butter
(not margarine, not unsalted butter)
1 cup white sugar
1 cup brown sugar
2 eggs
2 tablespoons real vanilla
3½ cups all purpose flour
1½ teaspoons baking soda
1 teaspoon salt
2 cups milk chocolate chips
2 cups semisweet chocolate chip
2 cups whole (not chopped) pecans or walnuts

Preheat oven to 350 degrees and prep cookie sheets with cooking spray.

Cream butter, brown sugar and white sugar until fluffy. Add eggs and vanilla, and beat well.

Add flour, baking powder and salt, and mix until combined. Mix in the chocolate chips, then gently add the nuts.

Use a #40 cookie scoop, or portion by spoonfuls to equal approximately 1½ tablespoons each.

Flatten each ball of dough somewhat. Bake approximately 12 minutes or until nicely browned on edges with lighter center. Let them rest on the cookie sheet for several minutes, then move them to a wire cooling rack.

COMING NEXT MONTH FROM
Love Inspired®

Available June 18, 2019

THE AMISH WIDOWER'S TWINS
Amish Spinster Club • by Jo Ann Brown

Leanna Wagler has barely gotten over Gabriel Miller standing her up and announcing he was marrying someone else when the widower and his twin babies move in next door. Now she's his temporary nanny, but can they finally reveal their secrets and become a forever family?

A LOVE FOR LIZZIE
by Tracey J. Lyons

When her father has a heart attack, Lizzie Miller's family needs help to keep their farm running, and her childhood friend, Paul Burkholder, volunteers. After a tragedy in the past, Lizzie withdrew from the community and Paul, but now she's finally dreaming of the future...and picturing herself by his side.

HEALING THE COWBOY'S HEART
Shepherd's Crossing • by Ruth Logan Herne

With his hands already full caring for his orphaned niece and nephew, cowboy Isaiah Woods finds a sick mare in foal. Now he must rely on the expertise of veterinarian Charlotte Fitzgerald to nurse the animal back to health, but will their business arrangement turn into something more?

WANDER CANYON COURTSHIP
Matrimony Valley • by Allie Pleiter

When his stepfather and her aunt get engaged, Chaz Walker and Yvonne Niles are sure it's a mistake. But will the surly cowboy and determined baker discover that the best recipe for love often includes the heart you least expect?

THE COWBOY'S FAITH
Three Sisters Ranch • by Danica Favorite

After being left at the altar, the last thing Nicole Bell wants is a reminder of her humiliation. But when Fernando Montoya—the brother of her former best friend who stole her fiancé—shows up, she can't avoid him...especially since he's the only person capable of helping her troubled horse.

HOMETOWN HOPE
by Laurel Blount

Five-year-old Jess Bradley hasn't spoken in the three years since her mother's death—until she begs her father, Hoyt Bradley, to stop a beloved bookstore from closing. Desperate to keep Jess talking, can Hoyt set aside a long-standing rivalry and work with Anna Delaney to save her floundering store?

———————

Get 4 FREE REWARDS!

We'll send you 2 FREE Books plus 2 FREE Mystery Gifts.

Love Inspired® books feature contemporary inspirational romances with Christian characters facing the challenges of life and love.

FREE Value Over $20

SPECIAL EXCERPT FROM

HQN™

*Read on for a sneak peek at
the second heartwarming book in
Lee Tobin McClain's Safe Haven series,*
Low Country Dreams!

Yasmin shifted on the glider, set it rocking with one foot and tucked the other foot up under her. The air was cooling now, a slight breeze bringing the fragrance of oleander flowers. It seemed only natural for Liam to shuffle closer on the glider. To let his arm curve around her shoulders.

Yasmin's breath whooshed out of her. Talking with Liam about her brother had made her feel vulnerable, but also relieved. Less alone. She remembered when she could share anything with Liam and he would always have her back. Such a wonderful feeling, especially after her brother had stopped being able to be that rock and that support to her.

Now Liam turned to meet her gaze head-on. His hand rose to brush back a curl that had escaped her ponytail. "I like your hairstyle," he said unexpectedly, his voice a tone deeper than usual. "Reminds me of the old days, when we were in school."

"In other words, I look like a kid?" Her words came out breathy, and she couldn't take her eyes off him.

Slowly, Liam shook his head. "Oh, no, Yasmin. You don't look like a kid at all." His eyes flickered down to her mouth, then back to her eyes.

Yasmin's heart fluttered like a terrified bird. Her stomach, her chest, all that was inside her felt squeezed by warm hands, melting.

How she wanted this. This opportunity to talk to Liam in a low, intimate voice. To feel that sense of promise, that there was something happy and bright in their future together.

She tried to grasp on to the reasons why this couldn't happen. How she didn't dare to have children, because the risk of them developing a mental illness was so high. Not only because of Josiah, although that was the main thing, of course. But also because of her mother's issues.

As if all of that wasn't enough, Yasmin knew she wasn't past the safe age herself. What if she got into a relationship and then started having delusions and hearing voices?

It was hard enough taking care of her brother, her blood relative. She owed him and bore the burden gladly. But she couldn't expect a romantic partner to do the same for her, wouldn't want someone to.

Wouldn't want Liam to.

If she let things go where they were headed right now, if she let him kiss her, she wasn't sure she would have the strength to push him away again. Doing it once had nearly killed her. Maybe she could be strong enough, but only if she put an end to this before getting closer. "I think we should go."

His head tilted to one side, his eyes steady on her. "Do you really think so?"

She hesitated, clung for just a moment to the possibility of not being the responsible one, the caretaker, the one who took charge of things and tried to make everything work out. She could let herself do what she wanted to do every now and then, couldn't she? She could be spontaneous, go with her emotions, her heart.

But no. Her duty was clear. Her life was about taking care of her family, not about indulging in something pleasurable for now, but ultimately dangerous to someone she cared about. Liam was too good of a man, had suffered too many of life's blows already, to be shackled with Yasmin's issues. "Yes," she said firmly. "I really think so."

Don't miss Lee Tobin McClain's
Low Country Dreams, *available June 2019*
wherever Harlequin® books and ebooks are sold.

www.Harlequin.com